Touch Him

Touch Him

The Man Trap Series
Book Three

By

Olivia Jaymes

www.OliviaJaymes.com

TOUCH HIM

Print Edition

Touch Him

Emerson Grant is practical, punctual, and incredibly efficient. Those qualities make her the perfect person to organize a fabulous wedding. She never gets caught up in the romance though. She's got her feet on the ground at all times.

Owen Campbell is known as Dr. Love. He owns the most successful dating site in the country. He believes there's someone out there for everyone, but he has yet to meet his own match.

Thrown together at a destination wedding, these two can barely agree on the color of the sky. But something funny happened on the way to the rehearsal dinner… Owen got a glimpse of the real Emmy. The one she barely shows to strangers. Now he wants to get to know her a whole lot better.

And show the cynical wedding planner the magic of love.

CHAPTER ONE

Emmy

WE WERE CHECKING each other out. I couldn't remember the last time something like this had happened to me. I didn't spend much time in bars and I spent even less looking at the male patrons, but this man wasn't someone I could easily ignore.

Sure, he was handsome, although not in that classic way. He was slightly too slim for societal standards, more like a lean swimmer's body, which I much preferred. His jaw wasn't as square as some other men but it was certainly firm, while his cheekbones were high and sharp. From this distance I couldn't see the color of his eyes but I could definitely tell that he held himself with a casual self-assurance that was extremely attractive.

He was chuckling at something the bartender said and it sounded warm and throaty. Genuine. I liked that.

There weren't many people in the hotel bar. The two of us, plus a table of four older men in the corner who had just finished a round of golf. It was probably only natural that we'd noticed each other. He was sitting at the bar and I'd chosen a table a few feet away. I was supposed to be meeting someone but he was running late. I, on the other hand, was on time. Something I prided myself on. Punctuality is a virtue.

I'd tried keeping my gaze straight in front of me and on my drink, a fruity concoction the bartender had recommended. It was cold, smooth, a little sharp, and it must have had a hell of a lot of rum because if I looked in a mirror, I was sure my cheeks would be bright pink.

But my tummy approved of the spicy cocktail and I took another sip, lifting my gaze ever so slightly – and hopefully surreptitiously – to check out Handsome Guy again.

Only this time he was looking back. Directly at me.

Our eyes met and for a moment I couldn't look away. Realizing that I'd been caught red-handed, I took a deep breath and stared down at my drink again. Much safer. My heart was still pounding and my palms sweaty at being found out.

But then again, he'd been looking, too. It's what we'd been doing for the last ten minutes, except not so blatantly. I could feel his gaze on my legs, bared by my sundress, and I had to resist the urge to tug at the suddenly too tight straps. It was really hot in this hotel. They needed to turn up the air conditioning, for heaven's sake. This was a tropical paradise and all but the humidity was out of control.

Taking another sip of my cool drink, I focused my gaze on the frosty glass in front of me and more specifically on the colorful pink umbrella balancing on the rim. I wasn't inexperienced when it came to the opposite sex, far from it, but I wasn't in the habit of picking up strange men in bars. He might be good-looking and it was fun to flirt a little, but I wasn't going to offer to buy him a drink or anything.

So far, although he'd looked me up and down, he hadn't

offered to buy me one, either. It looked like we were at a stalemate. We found each other attractive but we weren't going to do anything about it. I could live with that. I wasn't here for fun times. I was here to work and a sexy man who drank scotch neat would only be a distraction.

"Another, Dr. Campbell?" I heard the bartender ask.

So Handsome Guy was a doctor. What kind of doctor? Was he a doctor-doctor? Or a doctor of *something* like art history or world religions or archeology? Like Indiana Jones. If I suddenly passed out, would he be able to give me mouth to mouth?

But I wasn't going to pass out. I wasn't going to buy him a drink, and I wasn't going to introduce myself. I wasn't going to do any of those things.

Because I was here to work. Work. That thing that paid my bills. I was successful because I was damn good at my job and didn't lose focus. My clients were always happy. Or at least as happy as they could possibly be. I'd learned long ago that some people simply wanted to be miserable and take as many others with them as they could, like a drowning man pulling down their rescuer. I'd sworn that I wouldn't be one of them. After several years in the business I was also pretty damn good at figuring out who those people were ahead of time and pressing them to find a different event planner.

In other words, I had no problem firing a client. Frankly, life was too short to be unhappy.

Luckily for me and my wayward thoughts the party I was supposed to be meeting walked into the bar and slid into the chair opposite me. Daniel Drake, the groom of the destination wedding I was organizing here on the island. Nice man and totally besotted with his lovely bride-to-be. They were a great couple.

"Emerson," Daniel greeted me with a smile and a handshake. He was businesslike and I liked that about him. "Thank you for meeting with me on such short notice. I do appreciate it."

"It's no problem at all," I replied smoothly, as the handsome doctor stood from his barstool. He must be ready to leave. "How can I help you today?"

Instead of heading for the exit, the man lowered himself into a chair next to Daniel, who grinned and slapped him on the back. Uh oh. This wasn't good. At all.

"This is my friend, Dr. Owen Campbell, by the way," Daniel said as they relaxed back against the plush chairs. "He's my best man and is giving me a hand with the last-minute details. Owen, this is Emerson Grant."

The best man. The best man. *The best man.*

Thank goodness I hadn't tried to buy him a drink or something. I had a strict no fraternization policy when it came to those in the wedding party. Dr. Owen Campbell was off limits. An absolute no-go zone.

I didn't like the disappointment that made my cocktail taste suddenly sour. I hadn't had any plans to meet him so I shouldn't care either way.

Right?

As coolly as I could, I nodded to Owen Campbell. "It's nice to meet you, Doctor."

I congratulated myself on sounding calm and professional, which was exactly what I wanted to be. Not sweating with my stomach fluttering. Like a teenage girl.

"It's nice to meet you as well, Miss Grant." His eyes were a greenish-gold. "Please call me Owen."

"Call me Emmy," I replied automatically, dragging my gaze back to the groom. I wasn't here for the good doctor. "Now, how can I help you, Dan?"

"I want to give Lisa a really special bachelorette party tomorrow night. As you know she was supposed to have it last week but it had to be cancelled because of her work commitments. I don't want her to miss out on one of those major traditions." He grimaced and gave me a sheepish look. "I know it's last minute and I'll totally understand if you tell me no way, but is there any way that you can throw something together? It doesn't have to be big and flashy. No strippers or penis cakes. Just her friends, some booze, and maybe some dancing?"

Just to be clear, I didn't *throw things together* for a living. That's what other people did. The civilians. I was a general in the army of planning, organization, and fun. I could do a little better than some booze and music. In a way, I was disappointed in myself. I should have anticipated this since I was well aware of Lisa's work emergency.

"Of course, I can help you with this," I replied, keeping my attention on the groom. I could feel Owen Campbell's intent gaze on my face but I wouldn't give him the satisfaction of letting him know I noticed. "Did you want to invite all the female guests or just the wedding party?"

Dan launched into his list and I scribbled notes on the tablet that I carried everywhere, quite aware that the best man was watching my every move. A part of me wanted to stare right back and then make a funny face directly at him. The tension at the table was building but bless Dan, he appeared to be oblivious.

The back of my neck was hot, and I crossed and uncrossed my legs as I wrote down the last name on the guest list for Lisa's party. Thankfully, Dan hadn't lied. The roster of names wasn't that long. It would be a small and intimate affair.

"Okay, we have the list. Now, did you have any ideas for the party? Food or venue?"

Owen leaned forward, his forearms resting on the table. "We were hoping you'd have some thoughts."

"I absolutely do," I said, our gazes briefly colliding before I turned back to Dan. My fingers tightened on my tablet and I exhaled a shaky breath. Far safer over here. The mere closeness of this man was hell on my nerves. That rum drink wasn't sitting so easily in my stomach anymore. "If you think she'd like an outdoor party, there's a gorgeous canopied area near the south beach. If that's already booked, we can always use one of the empty suites."

I'd already spoken to the resort manager and he'd assured me there would be a few rooms as well for last minute guests.

"I really think she'd like it outdoors if you can arrange it," Dan enthused, turning to his best man. "What do you think?"

I found myself staring directly into those warm green eyes and a hot flush crawled up my chest. "I think that Miss Grant has this completely in hand. We should trust her."

Dan grinned again and nodded enthusiastically. "I absolutely do. I also trust you, which is why I asked you here to give me a hand. I don't want Lisa to get wind of this party. I want it to be a surprise. Can you work with Emmy on the details so that Lisa doesn't get suspicious? She'll wonder what's going on if I take a lot of calls or texts. I'd really appreciate it. I'm sure whatever you two decide will be perfect."

Ahh...wait. Did I get a vote? It didn't look like it.

Owen's lips twitched as he took the last sip of his scotch. "I'd be happy to. I'm sure that Miss Grant and I can pull something together for your bride. Just leave it to us."

Us. As in together.

It would seem that I wasn't going to be able to avoid Dr. Owen Campbell completely.

No problem. I could be cool, calm, and professional. This wasn't even a challenge. I had it all under control.

As always.

CHAPTER TWO

Owen

MY BUDDY DAN had excellent taste in event planners. Emerson Grant not only looked great, but she clearly knew what she was doing. In the twenty minutes she and I had been sitting at this table together she'd zipped through a planning checklist off the top of her head like a buzzsaw through wood.

That twenty minutes didn't count the ten minutes I'd spent eyeing her before Dan showed up. She wasn't tough to look at, by any means.

I wouldn't have described her as pretty. No, she was far too unconventional for such a wishy-washy term. But she was incredibly attractive in a sort of exotic way with her almond-shaped light blue eyes, golden skin, and long caramel colored hair. The rest of her was almost too good to be true as well. Those long, tanned legs alone weren't going to let me sleep peacefully tonight. It was a monument to how happy Dan was with Lisa that he'd never mentioned that their wedding planner was drop dead gorgeous.

Emmy tapped her tablet and pursed her lips. "I think that's everything. We've covered food, drinks, decorations, venue, music, and even a great cover story to keep it a secret until the last minute."

If anything, she was too efficient. She intrigued me and I wanted to spend more time with her. Was she as good on the inside as she was on the outside?

"There's nothing else?"

She shook her head and tucked the tablet computer into her large handbag. "That's it. Thank you for your help and being so decisive. It makes my job easier."

I signaled to the waiter for the check. "Let me pay the tab and then perhaps you can show me the venue. I'd really love to see it."

And spend more time with you.

She glanced at her watch and I was reminded that while I was on a short vacation for the weekend, Emmy was working.

"I won't keep you long. I know you're busy."

"Of course, I can show you the venue. It's a lovely location."

Quickly, before she changed her mind, I threw some cash on the table and stood. The clock was ticking and I only had a few minutes to get to know her better.

But I wasn't the smoothest motherfucker when it came to chatting up the ladies. I'd spent a chunk of my adult life doing research in a lab. I was no debonair playboy. I spent most nights alone and I was getting tired of it.

Placing her purse strap over her shoulder, Emmy stood as well. "It's just down the path. About a ten-minute walk."

That gave me twenty more minutes to get to know her.

We exited the back of the resort and headed down the narrow path to the south beach area. The afternoon was warm and humid and I could feel the sun on the back of my neck. The smell of chlorine and sunscreen hung in the air as we passed by the massive pool. The sound of laughter and splashing were barely muted by the music blaring from hidden speakers.

"Are you enjoying the sunny weather?"

Weather was lame opener but it was neutral. No way was I going to ask her who she'd voted for in the last election, although I wouldn't mind knowing that fact.

"I am," she replied, her shoulders relaxing slightly as we walked. Maybe a non-controversial question had been a good gambit after all. "It's freezing back in Illinois, although I don't mind the cold weather normally. I like sweaters and fireplaces. Hot chocolate and snow."

The path took a turn away from the resort and the music faded into the background. "I think I like summer the best," I said. "Swimming. Hiking. Camping."

Wow, I was so freaking articulate and interesting. Not. I needed to up my game and fast.

"Do you like the outdoors, Emmy?"

By the way she hesitated, I could tell the answer was no but she was trying to find a nice way to say it.

"I'd consider myself to be more of a homebody."

I was rarely at home. My house always felt too large, too quiet, and too empty.

"What do you like to do…at home?"

"I read a lot. Work. Have friends over. Watch 'The Walking Dead'. Just like everyone else."

I'd never seen a single episode of 'The Walking Dead'. I wasn't against the idea of zombies but I'd never really understood the allure, either.

Books. We had books in common.

"I love to read. What are your favorites?"

"I'm a fan of mysteries. Currently I'm working through all of Agatha Christie. What about you?"

"Science fiction mostly, but I also read horror and thrillers as well."

So intent I was on our discussion I hadn't noticed that we'd arrived at our destination. Nestled on a low hill overlooking the beach, the venue was an open-air structure reminiscent of a gazebo but much larger. It could easily accommodate a party of twenty and there were only ten people on Dan's guest list.

"I think Lisa will love this. How did you even know about it?"

Emmy laughed at my amazement. "It's my job to know."

"You've been here before?"

"I have. I did a fiftieth anniversary a few years ago. The couple renewed their vows on the beach and then had a small reception here with their children and a few friends."

"That's a wonderful story. You must see a great deal of love and happiness in your job. It must be quite rewarding."

"It is, although I do my share of divorce parties as well."

I walked over to the edge of the hill and looked out onto the sparkling blue water. There was something about the pull and push of the water on the sand that soothed all the stresses that I'd brought with me from civilization.

"Surely they're the exception and not the rule?"

"They are," Emmy conceded, joining me to look out over the strip of sandy paradise. "But not every wedding or anniversary is full of love and romance. Sometimes it appears to me as if people are just going through the motions."

"That's sad. They shouldn't settle for anything less than the real thing."

I wasn't going to, either. I'd wait until I found the right woman. It didn't appear that Emerson Grant was that female, though. I'd have to keep looking.

Whether she agreed with my sentiment was a mystery because she didn't reply, instead sweeping am arm toward the far end of the pavilion.

"I was thinking we'd set up the buffet on that end and the DJ over there. Dan said that Lisa and her friends liked to dance. They're going to have so much fun."

I nodded in agreement. "It sounds like it. How can you get a DJ on such short notice?"

"The resort sort of has one. He's mostly a waiter but he has DJ equipment if needed for emergencies."

"An emergency DJ. Who knew there was such a thing? Do we need to provide him a music list?"

Emmy shook her head. "I used Dan and Lisa's reception music list as a starting point. Took out 'The Chicken Dance' and added a few more dance tunes."

I tried to hide my wince but apparently, I wasn't fast enough. Emmy's brow raised in question. "Which one do you hate? 'The Chicken Dance' or dance music?"

"Neither. Well...both, actually. I'm not a fan of most modern dance music. I like a nice slow ballad for dancing and jazz for listening."

"I don't know much about jazz."

"I could recommend some."

"Um, that's okay. I don't get to listen to much music anyway. Usually just at wedding receptions and parties."

In other words, she hated jazz. Another item where we differed. Clearly the only thing we had in common was this wedding. Too bad.

Emmy glanced at her watch and then toward the resort. "Thank you for the help but I really do need to be going. I have quite a bit of work to do to put together the details for Lisa's party. Do you have any more questions or concerns?"

"You seem to have everything well in hand."

She was damn good at her job. I had to give her that. Competence was sexy.

"I think that I do. If I have any more questions, I'll contact you."

There wouldn't be any more reasons for us to spend time together and that was fine. There might be a spark between us but eventually we had to talk to each other. "That sounds fine. Thanks for showing me the venue."

"It was no trouble."

I bid goodbye to Emerson Grant, feeling a pang of regret as I watched her walk away. Beautiful woman, but we weren't compatible in the least.

★ ★ ★

AWKWARD. IT WAS the only way to describe my time with Owen Campbell.

We didn't have a damn thing in common other than we found each other physically attractive. At least I assumed he did from the way he'd looked at me. I certainly found him yummy but it had been so hard to talk to him. We didn't have much to chat about other than the two people who connected us – Dan and Lisa.

I'd checked off the last item on today's to-do list and headed back to my room. Kicking off my shoes, I fell back on the bed and checked my text messages.

One from my mom.

One from my friend Mia who was currently residing in Scotland.

One from my friend Ashlyn.

Mia and Ashlyn were part of my friend circle, along with Mia's older sister Shelby. The four of us were a tightknit group and more like family than friends. I'd trust them with my life and my secrets. If I had any secrets.

I pressed Ashlyn's contact and her phone rang a few times before she answered.

"It's fifteen degrees here."

"And a hello to you, too," I laughed. "Is that any way to answer your phone?"

"It is when one of my best friends in the world is sunning herself in the tropical Caribbean. Tell me all about it. I can live vicariously through you. Is it warm? Can you feel the sun on your skin?"

Ashlyn knew better than this so it must be really fucking cold back home.

"You know that I'm not on vacation. I'm working. I am not

lying in the sun ordering drinks from a handsome cabana guy. I'm working my tail off here."

"Is it warm?" Ashlyn persisted. "Tonight the wind chill is supposed to be zero."

Normally, I really like winter weather but even I had to admit that it was getting old. It was time for spring.

"It is warm," I admitted. "Very warm. Hot, really. And my hair is curling because of the humidity."

"I don't feel sorry for you in the least," Ashlyn replied, her tone tart. "Did I mention that it's supposed to snow here? Again. We may never see the ground at this rate."

"It does always feel like that this time of year, doesn't it?" I laughed. "But summer does always come and then you're complaining about the heat."

"I never complain about the heat."

"You do."

"I have no memory of what you're talking about. You must be delirious…from the *heat* there. Now tell me about how the wedding plans are going. It should all be on cruise control by now."

Normally, it would be and the only work I'd need to do would be to make sure what was supposed to happen actually did happen.

"Groom threw me a last-minute curve ball. The bachelorette party last week was cancelled due to the bride's work commitments. Her entire office got the flu and she was practically the only one standing. He wanted to give her a surprise bachelorette party tomorrow night, so I've been working on that today."

"No rest for you, then. Is it going to happen?"

Of course. I made dreams come true. At least that's what my business card said.

"It is." I paused for a moment, not sure whether to mention Owen but something was pushing me to do it. "The groom lent me his best man to help with the preparations. You know…answer questions and such. That way he wouldn't be getting texts from me and it wouldn't raise any suspicions with the bride."

"Is he?"

I didn't have a clue as to what Ashlyn was talking about.

"Is he what?"

"The best man."

Oh.

"Why do you ask?"

Delay and deny.

"Because you sounded strange when you mentioned him. So give it up, girl. What gives? Is he gorgeous? He is, isn't he? Tell me every little detail and don't leave anything out, especially the really salacious stuff."

"I'm working, Ash. There is no salacious stuff. That's my rule, and I never break rules."

"But there is something going on. Spill it."

"It's not a big deal."

"It was enough for you to mention."

I did, didn't I?

"There's this man–"

"I'm listening," Ashlyn interrupted. "Is he handsome? I bet he is."

"Who's telling this story?" I teased my friend. "If you already know it, then I don't have to tell you."

"Sorry, keep going."

"So there's this man," I began again. "And yes, he is handsome. Quite good-looking. Sexy."

"What's he look like?"

"Dark hair. Nice eyes. Keeps in shape. He's a doctor, too."

"Oh," Ashlyn breathed. "A doctor. A real one? Or like Shelby?"

Our friend Shelby had a PhD in psychology, so she was a real doctor, just not a medical one.

"Don't let Shelby hear you say that. As for what kind he is, I don't know. I only heard him addressed as Doctor. He could be either one. Honestly, I don't care which. Either way he's extremely accomplished and probably intelligent, too."

"Handsome and successful. A powerful combination. So what's the problem? Is he married?"

"I don't think so. There's no ring."

That didn't mean he was single, though. I was making assumptions based on how he'd looked at me, which in hindsight was rather naive. Married men looked at women.

"Emmy, you're dancing around here. What's going on with this guy?"

"We don't have a thing in common. Not one thing except this wedding."

There. I'd said it out loud.

"How do you even know?"

"I was showing him the venue for the bachelorette party," I explained with a groan. "We got to talking. He's one of those people that likes hot weather, jazz, and the outdoors. Dear heavens, Ash…he goes *camping*. Like outside. On purpose."

My distaste for the great outdoors was well known among my friends and family. There were bugs and dirt and no plumbing. Maybe snakes and bears, too. S'mores simply weren't enough of a benefit to compensate for all the negatives.

I could hear Ashlyn's laughter through the phone.

"So glad I could entertain you," I said, acid in my tone. "With friends like you–"

"Okay, calm down. It is kind of funny though, if you think about it. You meet some great guy and he's like some Outward Bound dude. Does he climb mountains, too?"

Ashlyn's boyfriend Kyle had climbed a mountain once.

"I don't know and I wouldn't care as long as he didn't want to drag me along with him."

"Maybe he doesn't care if you go camping, either," Ashlyn suggested. "Maybe he only goes with his guy friends. Like a male bonding kind of event."

"Maybe…"

Except I kind of got the idea that he hoped that I would like it too by the way he'd said it. As if he wanted me to jump in and say how much I loved camping as well.

"But why does it matter? You're only just getting to know each other. You know, in Shelby's book it talks about how differences are good and that you shouldn't try to date yourself, basically. Being with someone the same would be boring."

Glancing down at my carryon bag, I could see the corner of the blue binder sticking out. Shelby's book. I'd promised to read it and I always kept my promises.

"You didn't think disagreeing was so great when you met

Kyle," I reminded her. "You hated his guts."

"And I was wrong," she replied. "We're actually more alike than we are different. The most important is morals, values, and goals. Those are the same. As for whether he hates rom-coms or I hate thrillers…that's minor. We simply compromise every now and then. For example, the other day we went for Thai food even though Kyle hates Thai food. So later I let him pick the movie. Compromise."

"I don't want to eat food I don't like."

Outdoors. With no bathroom.

"He found a dish on the menu that he was okay with. He didn't hate it. When you fall in love, you'll want to make compromises."

I'd heard that before from couples in love. They were probably right which could only mean one thing.

I'd never been in love.

Not really. Just flimsy facsimiles. It didn't say much for my taste in men. Or me, for that matter. Perhaps I was one of those people that didn't inspire love. Or compromise, for that matter. I might be destined to be alone for the rest of my life, except for a bunch of cats.

Wait…I'm allergic to cats. Could I be a crazy dog lady instead? Did they allow that? How about fish? With my busy schedule I could probably take care of an aquarium.

"I'm sure I will," I finally replied. "But until then I'm not going camping. It doesn't matter, anyway. He's a member of the wedding party which means he's off limits. No going there."

"You really need to read the book."

"I will. In fact, I'll order room service and read some of it tonight."

"Excellent."

"Right after the welcome cocktail party."

"Em," Ashlyn sighed. "Do you even ever sleep?"

"I'll sleep when I'm dead."

"If you don't slow down, that may be sooner rather than later."

Less time to be a crazy cat lady then.

"If I make it through the night, I'll call you tomorrow."

"Read the book," Ashlyn said as I ended the call.

Pulling it out of my bag, I threw it down on the bed and glared at it.

"You're a pain in the ass, you know that?"

The book didn't answer, of course, but it did sort of lie there...mocking me. It had the upper hand at this moment because I'd promised.

Tonight, I was going to keep that promise. But first I had to attend a party and avoid Dr. Owen Campbell.

How difficult could it be?

CHAPTER THREE

Emmy

I HAD SHELBY'S book spread across one side of the bathroom vanity and my makeup on the other, reading snippets as I applied mascara. I'd learned to multi-task years ago and I swear it's the key to getting shit done.

The book was actually pretty damn good. My friend had made massive revisions after Mia and Ashlyn had read through it. In her first draft, the beginning was a tad old-fashioned for me but now it read far more contemporary. The tone was extremely empowering and I appreciated the practical, down to earth step by step relationship advice.

Honestly, most of it seemed like common sense.

It wasn't rocket science to dump a guy if he never called. Or if he showed up late for every date. Or didn't show up at all without a good reason, like a car accident. I wouldn't have much heartburn about breaking up with a man if he constantly talked to his ex-girlfriend and was going over to her house several times a week. But I was the type that didn't take much crap when I dated.

Which might be why I'm single. Hey, I'm fine with it. I'd rather be alone than with the wrong man.

Tonight was the welcome cocktail party for family and others who were in the wedding. It was a small, intimate affair and the wedding party had come in early, wanting to get out of the cold and snow back home.

Twisting the mascara tube closed, I surveyed my lipstick choices. As an event planner I normally tried to blend into the decor, not taking any attention from the real stars of the show – the bride and groom. Tonight would be no different. I was wearing a simple black halter dress and black high-heeled sandals. If I'd been going out with the girls I would have chosen a red shade, but this was for work. A pink-beige nude would do the job. Quickly I swiped it on and checked my teeth for any transfer.

Satisfied that I didn't look a fright, I tossed the book on the bed and grabbed my evening bag. I wanted to be the first person downstairs in case there were any issues. Not that I expected any. This resort was first class and had been on top of every single request.

I pushed open my door and stepped into the hallway just as the door next to mine opened too.

Owen.

He was in the room next to mine? How did I not know that? Clearly, I was slipping as I was supposed to know all the details of this wedding.

Crap. It was going to be more difficult to avoid him if he was staying only a few feet from me.

"Miss Grant."

He looked good, dressed in a blue suit and blue and gold tie. Despite the casual vibe of the island and resort, Lisa and Dan had asked their wedding party to dress up for the event tonight.

So he's handsome. So what? Lots of men were good-looking.

"Dr. Campbell."

"Please call me Owen."

"Then you should call me Emmy."

We'd done this once before in the bar and it was even more awkward a second time. He shut his door with a loud click and slipped his key card into the breast pocket of his jacket. He had nice hands. Long fingers. Maybe he was a surgeon.

"Headed to the party?"

I nodded and tucked my bag under my arm. "I am. I wanted to be there early."

And I wouldn't be if I didn't get a move on. I hated to be late.

"That's where I'm going too. Dan asked us guys to be there early as well. He wants to talk to us about tomorrow night."

"The bachelorette party?"

Owen's smile widened. "Specifically, what we're going to do while the ladies party. I voted for beer and pizza."

"That sounds like a very wise choice as long as you don't drink too much."

Geez, I sounded like someone's uptight mother.

"We'll keep Dan on the straight and narrow." Owen held out his arm indicating that I should go ahead. He fell into step beside me. I wasn't going to be able to shake him until we arrived at the party. "We don't want him hung over and miserable for his own wedding, but a couple of beers won't hurt."

The elevator doors slid open as if they'd been waiting for us.

"You're a doctor. You don't know some amazing hangover cure?"

"I'm not that kind of doctor. But I do think that lots of water doesn't hurt. Honestly, I think my last hangover was back in college."

My last hangover was about three months ago. Too much wine. Another item we didn't have in common.

I kept my mouth shut during the elevator ride. I'd been determined to avoid him but the universe was clearly messing with me.

"How's the planning for the bachelorette party? Is there anything you need my help with?"

This man could not take a hint. I'd been studiously avoiding even looking at him hoping he'd ignore me as well, but he just didn't get it.

"It's fine. It's all set. No worries."

Now I just sounded bitchy. Not what I was going for. Time to reset.

"But I do appreciate the offer. It really is all set."

The doors slid open and I practically jumped out of the car but Owen – with those long legs – was right behind me. Damn. A girl couldn't catch a break tonight.

"How do you plan to get Lisa out to the venue? I might be able to help there."

I wanted to smack myself in the forehead and then do the same to Owen. Did he not see that I was desperately trying to get away from him? I'd done everything but burrow a hole in the floor beneath my feet and cover myself with dirt and tile.

"It's all taken care of. I'll call Lisa to tell her I found the perfect spot to have some wedding photos taken and I need her to see it."

I stopped just outside the entrance to the bar where the party would take place. It was perfect for the event and had a fantastic patio that overlooked the beach. We had it all to ourselves tonight from five to seven.

Nice. Be nice. Patient. He's a nice man. He could have been a real asshole.

"I appreciate so much all the assistance you've given me, Owen. It was very kind of you to help your friend out. If I need anything else, I'll let you know but I truly think it's all set up. You should just relax and enjoy your weekend."

He simply nodded, his gaze going over my shoulder. I could hear Dan and Lisa arriving behind me. "I'm sure you have it all in hand. Have a nice evening."

Just like that he moved past me to meet his friends. Breathing a sigh of relief, I entered the bar and ordered a drink. I had to do better at avoiding this man.

This incredibly sexy man.

★ ★ ★

Owen

DAN AND I sat at a corner of the bar as the guests trickled in one by one. We were both nursing a beer and munching on the most delicious pigs in a blanket that I'd ever tasted. I should have expected it, though. Emmy the Efficient would of course have found a chef that could make hot dogs and dough taste amazing.

I dunked my dog into the mustard dollop on my tiny plate.

"All I'm saying is that your wedding planner is tightly wound."

Dan just laughed and took a long draw from his beer. "She's in charge of this entire event and it has to go off without a hitch. What did you expect?"

"I just expected her to be different."

What in the ever-loving fuck was I even talking about? I didn't know. I guess I'd simply expected a wedding planner to be more romantic and starry-eyed, instead of like General Patton.

"She's never been anything but wonderful to me and Lisa. Always nice and polite. Really caring about us getting the wedding that we want." He rubbed his chin, a shit-eating grin on his face. "I'm going to go out on a limb here and guess that she wasn't terribly impressed by you. Did you take a one-two punch straight to the ego, my friend?"

"It's not like that," I replied quickly, although it kind of was. Emmy couldn't wait to get rid of me a few minutes ago. It was like I'd had the Black Plague. "I didn't ask her out if that's what you're thinking."

"I'm thinking you found her attractive – which she is – and the feeling wasn't returned."

She'd been cold as ice. I'd expected to see penguins waddling behind her.

"I'm interested in a hell of a lot more than a woman's looks. She has to be the whole package."

Dan wagged a finger at me. "That's your problem. You're looking for perfection."

"I am not looking for perfection," I objected. "Far from it. I just want a woman to want to be in a relationship. Miss Grant seems a bit…chilly and distant. Prickly. There's no romance in her soul. I doubt she's ever been in love."

I sounded like I knew her even though I'd only talked to her twice. What was I going on and on about?

"Maybe you can take her out into the moonlight and show her the error of her ways."

That was never going to happen.

"Are you kidding? She'd rip me limb from limb. That's a woman that doesn't gaze at stars or walk in the rain. All I'd get is a lecture about how we'd both catch pneumonia."

Emerson Grant simply wasn't my type. No worries. There were plenty of fish in the sea. Just none that looked like her.

"Come on, she's not that bad. Maybe she's seen too much to be all starry-eyed."

"Like what?"

He shrugged. "I dunno. Grooms getting caught doing the maid of honor. Brides running off with the best man. Feuding couples. Gold diggers of either sex. Divorces before the ink is dry on the license. Giver her a break, man. Not all of your couples make it, either."

That was true. But…

Lisa sidled up to Dan and he wrapped an arm around her waist. "Honey, don't you think Owen and Emerson would make a great couple?"

Oh shit. I wanted to punch Dan right then and there but then he'd have a black eye for his own damn wedding. Lisa would kill me.

"We would not–"

"Yes!" Lisa exclaimed, her eyes lighting up. She clapped her hands together and practically jumped up and down with glee.

Because she was happy in love, she wanted everyone to be happy in love. Plus, she knew that I wanted to settle down eventually. "You two would look so cute together. You should ask her to dance. Or get her a drink."

Giving Dan a nasty look, I now had the task of getting out of this. "Definitely not. We're not each other's type."

Lisa waggled her eyebrows. "She's very attractive."

Incredibly. Too beautiful.

"And she's working. I don't think she'd appreciate me interrupting that."

Her mouth turned down, Lisa sighed loudly. "We just want you to be as happy as we are. If it weren't for you, Dan and I wouldn't have found each other."

That was true. They'd met through my dating website. They'd taken the personality and interests test and been matched with one another.

"I like to think that the two of you were destined for each other and would have met no matter what."

"Awww, that's so sweet." Lisa stood on her tiptoes and dropped a brief kiss on my cheek. "We need to find you a really nice woman."

The irony of a man who owned a dating site not being able to find the right woman wasn't lost on me. In fact, it was downright sad, and more than a little frustrating. But tonight wasn't about me.

"I'm really okay. Now how about we have a toast to the happy couple?"

CHAPTER FOUR

Emmy

DAN AND LISA were up to something and being none too sly about it.

Wearing matching smirks, they'd called me over and asked me several questions, all of which they already knew the answers to. Then they'd grabbed Owen from a group of people he was talking with and dragged him into the conversation as well.

Could they be… Were they *matchmaking*? Holy hell. I didn't get involved with the wedding party – ever – though I'd been sorely tempted when I'd first seen Owen and didn't know who he was. Now that I did I wasn't going down that road, especially as I'd found out we didn't have much in common.

Or anything at all. Conversation had been difficult at best.

"We had a question about the rented tuxes," Lisa said, after pulling me over for the third time. "After the wedding, should the men return them individually or is there a central location to drop them off?"

We'd gone over this but Dan and Lisa were such a sweet couple I couldn't get impatient with them. "All they have to do is hang them in the closet in their hotel room. The staff will take it from there."

"Perfect," Lisa exclaimed, a big smile on her face. "Did you hear that? It's one of my favorites. Emmy, do you like this song?"

A love ballad from the eighties. I listened to the oldies station quite a bit at home.

"I do. It's one of my favorites also."

Lisa linked her arm with Dan's. "Let's dance. Owen, you should ask Emmy to dance, too."

I'd been outmaneuvered. I hadn't been paying enough attention, so now I was being led onto the dance floor by Owen because to refuse would have been churlish and rude. Well, damn.

When he placed his hand at the small of my back, I took in a whiff of his body wash or aftershave. He smelled good. Like he'd just stepped out of the shower, which I loved. But it also gave me an image of how he might look doing just that… Naked and wet.

I could feel the heat rise in my cheeks as I ruthlessly pushed the picture out of my head.

Bad. Very bad, Emmy. Be a professional. Not a pervert.

Since this was really just a bar, the dance floor wasn't large, just about the size of a postage stamp. About a dozen couples crowded into the small space which meant that Owen and I were pressed together whether I liked it or not.

And I did like it. Dammit.

I could feel the length of his body against me, the warmth of his skin under my palms through the cotton of his button down shirt, his breath tickling my ear. He'd taken off his suit jacket at some point. I was hyper aware, possibly more than I ever had been in my life before this moment. Every rise and fall of his chest, every movement of his muscles, every flicker of his ridiculously long eyelashes.

Owen was all around me, taking up all the oxygen in the space. It made me anxious and fidgety and I accidentally stepped on his toes which then had me apologizing. The earth could open up and swallow me at any moment. That'd be fine and dandy.

"Sorry," I said again when another dancer bumped into me, sending me even closer to his muscled frame. Solid. I tried to put some space between us but there was literally no room. "It's really crowded."

His gaze went over my head to the French doors that led to the back patio. "I don't know about you but I could use some fresh air."

Air. That sounded like heaven. I needed to breathe. The attraction to this man was stronger than I'd realized. He was tempting. I'd need to be vigilant, never letting my guard down. First thing? Put some damn distance between us as soon as possible. A girl could only take so much. I wasn't made of stone.

I don't remember answering him in the affirmative but I must have, because now we were standing in a corner of the back patio overlooking the beach. The palm trees swayed in the gentle breeze and even from this distance I could hear the soft lap of the water against the sand.

"I never sleep better than when I'm near the ocean," Owen said, leaning an elbow on the railing, completely at ease while I was a freakin' mess. "It's so hypnotic, the push and pull of the tide."

He had a poetic, romantic side. One I didn't possess. Most

of the time I didn't think about it much or care, but at moments like this one I wished that I pretty words, too.

But I didn't.

"It is beautiful here."

I was known for my efficiency, not my eloquence.

"How long have you been an event planner, Emmy?"

Now this was a subject I had the words for.

★ ★ ★

Owen

MOST PEOPLE LOVED talking about their work and I prayed that this would be the case. There had been tension between the two of us this evening, especially on the dance floor. Emmy had held herself so stiffly, she'd barely been able to move to the music.

And that was saying something because I danced like a department store mannequin.

"Right out of college, actually. Luckily, I was too young and dumb to know that you shouldn't open your open business with no money and only ambition, but it ended up working out. It's been ten years now and I've built a solid business with an excellent reputation."

She was a hard worker with goals. Maybe even a little bit of a dreamer.

"Yours was the only name that Dan and Lisa had for a wedding planner," I offered. "They never spoke about anyone else."

It was the truth.

Emmy's cheeks turned a becoming shade of pink. "That's lovely. They're such a wonderful couple. Working with them has been fun. How about you, Owen? What do you do for a living?"

"I also own my own business."

"What kind of business?"

I really should be better at answering this question. I'd done it a million times but it never seemed to get any easier. I should have been prepared. I'd asked her about her profession, so of course she was going to ask about mine.

"I own a dating website."

She turned to look up at me, her brows furrowed. "A dating website," she echoed. "I'm not sure I follow you."

"*Symphonic*," I replied, swallowing a sigh. Clearly, she was not impressed. "It's called *Symphonic*. I use a researched and tested set of questions to find the perfect match for a client. I developed it myself."

"I've heard of it," she replied, her gaze back on the deserted beach. "I've seen the commercials."

Definitely not impressed.

"I thought you were a doctor," she finally said when I didn't say anything right away.

Not this again. My own family didn't think I was a *real* doctor.

"I am a doctor. I have a PhD in psychology. I've worked in research and also had a private practice for a few years. I've written three books about relationships."

"But your dream was to run a dating site?"

Emerson Grant made it sound like I was cooking meth in my kitchen.

"My dream as a researcher was to figure out how to help people find true love. I set out to learn as much about the emotion as I possibly could. How do people fall in love? Why do they fall in love or out of it, for that matter? Can love truly last a lifetime? I'd seen so many people in my private practice in real pain. People want to be in love. They *need* to be in love. It's what fulfills us in the end when the world lets us down."

Okay, maybe I'd gone a little far there but I truly believed it. It was a subject I was passionate about and I'd spent years studying love and people.

"I'm not sure people actually need to be in love," Emmy replied, clearing her throat. "It's not like water or air. They may want love but they don't need it."

"I beg to differ. I think that they do. It may not be like air and water but I think the human soul craves connections."

"You're a romantic."

She didn't make it sound like a positive trait.

"I am," I agreed readily. "And you're not, I take it?"

Leaning against the railing, a breeze caught a few strands of her hair and they clung to her cheek. I had to resist the urge to smooth them back. From what I was learning about this female, she wasn't for me. No matter how beautiful she was.

"I would consider myself practical. Down to earth. Rational."

Interesting.

"You don't think a person can be both practical and romantic at the same time? They're mutually exclusive?"

Her laugh was rich and warm. "I think that they are. You don't?"

"I think I can be romantic about love and practical about other things. I don't run around in the rain and catch pneumonia. I don't spend money I don't have. I don't set goals and then don't work toward them so yes, I do think a person can be both."

"I would guess that you're more practical than you realize."

That statement made me smile. "You think I believe that I'm romantic but I'm not really?"

"Well…yes."

"What is your definition of a romantic, Emmy?"

She turned, her brows pulled down in thought. "Byron was a romantic. Van Gough was a romantic."

"So if I cut off my ear and write poetry then I'm romantic?"

"That's not what I meant."

"I think I get what you're saying. You think that if someone is romantic then they're that way in their life completely."

Sighing, Emmy checked her watch. "If you want to consider yourself romantic, Owen, then you most certainly can. I wouldn't think my opinion one way or another would sway your thoughts."

"They won't." But I couldn't help but poke the bear a bit. Emmy Grant was intelligent and professional but a tad prickly. "I just find it strange that you plan weddings for a living but you don't seem all that into love and romance."

"I plan *events* for a living. Some of them just happen to be weddings. And I think love and romance are just wonderful." She looked up at me and her eyes narrowed. "Are you saying you think I'm cynical?"

A little.

"I don't think it matters what I think," I returned, echoing her own words. "It's just a surprise that you said that love was a want and not a need," I replied, referring back to our earlier conversation. "I would imagine you see people desperately in love every day."

"I do but that doesn't mean that love is a need. People don't die from not having love."

"I disagree. Haven't you ever heard of someone dying from a broken heart?"

"Yes, but I'm sure there's a perfectly rational medical reason for their passing. It's not really a broken heart."

"There are well documented cases of people dying from a broken heart when nothing else is medically wrong with them."

"I haven't really done any research on this subject so I'll have to take your word for it."

"I have done my research, I assure you. I've helped people find the love of their lives, including Dan and Lisa. Sadly, I haven't been as lucky. Not yet, anyway. But I will be. The magic of love is not something I want to miss out on."

"Magic," she repeated as if trying on the word for size. "The magic of love?"

I understood now.

"You don't think love is magic," I said flatly. "You don't believe in it."

Emerson Grant had never been in love.

"Let's just agree to disagree. I think love is wonderful but it's not some magic cure-all."

"You don't want to find your soulmate?"

I wanted to find mine and I didn't think I was less masculine because of it.

"I'm not sure I believe in the concept of soulmates. That one perfect person on the planet that completes you in a way that no one else can."

"I'm not sure that there's only one person," I explained. "I'd like to think that there are many but the odds are stacked against us finding them."

"And that's where your dating app comes in?"

Unlike most people, Emmy wouldn't be begging me to use my dating site to help her find a match. She made it sound a little sordid and dirty.

"It does. I help people find prospective matches with persons they may never have looked twice at in a bar, for example."

"By taking a compatibility test?"

"It's more than that but it's okay if you want to characterize it that way. Yes, they take a test about themselves and what's important to them. I would think someone as practical and down to earth as yourself would like the idea of finding a mate in such an efficient and straightforward manner."

I was probably going to hell for that statement.

Her lips tightened. "I guess I'm just not a big fan of dating apps."

Or their CEOs.

"Fair enough. It's not everyone's cup of tea."

Glancing over her shoulder to the French doors that led inside, she tucked her tiny purse under her arm. "Thank you for the fresh air but I really do need to check on the wait staff and the appetizer buffet. I hope you have a nice evening, Owen."

With that, she turned on her heel and marched back into the bar, leaving me standing on the patio. So much for Lisa and Dan's matchmaking skills. Emmy Grant might be beautiful but she didn't think much of me. Which left me to wonder…

If she took my *Symphonic* test, just what kind of man would she be matched with?

CHAPTER FIVE

Emmy

"THEY CALL HIM Dr. Love," Shelby said in that disapproving tone she was so known for. "Dr. Owen Campbell is one of the most preeminent researchers in the field of human relationships. In. The. World. He's authored three textbooks and I'm told he's working on a non-academic book for the masses. He's not a hack, Emmy. He's considered to be brilliant in his field. If he wrote a forward for my book, I would think I'd died and gone to heaven."

"So you know him?"

"I wouldn't call us close friends but we have a professional relationship. He lives in Arborville."

After my run-in with Owen Campbell I'd returned to my hotel room so that I could collapse after the long day. I needed a hot bath and a glass of wine. Maybe some room service, too.

"He's an expert in the field of love? There's actually people studying that?"

I don't know why I asked because I had a feeling I wasn't going to like the answer.

"There's lots of people studying that and Owen Campbell is head and shoulders above the rest. He knows his stuff."

"He runs a dating website, Shelby. You don't think that's more than a little bit cheesy?"

"It's not about hooking up for a one-night stand," my friend argued. "It's about finding the love of your life. He uses a researched and tested methodology to match people. He had great success even before he started the website. He was doing it in the lab at a major university."

Well…shit.

"It sounds like voodoo," I muttered, my head falling back on my pillow. I was lying on the bed in just my cocktail dress, my shoes kicked off somewhere near the door. I'd called Shelby immediately, not bothering to do anything first except flop on the mattress. "You can't find love that way."

"I would think you of all people, Emmy, would appreciate his approach," Shelby argued. "It's practical and efficient. All the things you love."

Owen had said the exact same thing and they both had a point. Why did I have a problem with this?

"He sounds like a crackpot," I shot back. "You should hear him talk about soulmates and true love. He says he's a romantic."

There was silence on the other end of the phone. Shelby rarely didn't have anything to say so I could only conclude that she was deciding which burning comeback she was going to use on me.

"You don't believe in soulmates?"

What was it with people today? Why was my belief system on trial?

"Maybe…I don't know. If you're asking if I believe there's

one and only one person in the world for me then...no. I don't believe in soulmates. Why? Do you?"

Shelby was almost – not quite – but almost as practical as I was. I considered her one of the smartest people I knew and I valued her counsel.

"I'd like to, wouldn't you? Don't you want to believe in a man destined just for you?"

"I'd like to believe in Santa and unicorns too but that would be futile, Shelby. We need to be–"

"Practical," she finished for me. "Yes, I know. But it's fun to think about, isn't it?"

"Is Brad your soulmate?"

It was a shitty question to ask. All of Shelby's friends had issues with him. He was a nice guy, but if that was her soulmate then she needed to talk to whomever was in charge of assigning them. If I had a damn soulmate he'd better be more attentive and he better dance with me in the goddamn rain or some shit like that. I'd want him to break into song like in the movies.

That wasn't going to happen. Because...reality. A highly underrated concept.

"Having a soulmate doesn't mean they're perfect," Shelby replied, in a far more reasonable tone than I deserved. "You're confusing a man that makes everything better with a man that is faultless and frankly doesn't exist. Even a practical woman such as yourself can admit that there might be a person out that that makes your day happier and brighter."

"There might."

"I think we're getting somewhere. Now tell me what you said to Owen. Do you owe him an apology, Emmy?"

Probably. I hadn't been very nice, but then he'd been a bit preachy about love and soulmates and all of that stuff.

"He might owe me one. Did you ever think of that?"

A loud sigh. Shelby was losing patience with me. I didn't blame her.

"You questioned his life's work. His integrity as a scientist. That's not nice."

It wasn't and I did feel guilty. He seemed to be a perfectly nice person who had a strange career. That didn't make him a bad person. Although…

"He sells dreams to people, Shel," I argued, not ready to give up yet. "He gets their hopes up and sells them snake oil, basically."

"Which part of *researched and tested* did you not understand? This is not snake oil. You should sign up and see what it's about. Worst case scenario you realize it's not voodoo and best case you might find the man of your dreams."

If I wasn't so tired I'd laugh. "Me? Sign up on a dating website? You have to be joking. Have you had a recent blow to the head?"

"I have not," she responded tartly. "I think you should find out more before you dismiss it all out of hand. You know…there's a chapter in my book about dating websites and *Symphonic* is my recommendation. But you wouldn't know that because you haven't read it yet."

It was my turn to sigh. "I did start to read it last night. I promised to read it and I will. I mean it, Shel. I'll read it. But I won't get far this weekend. I'm working. This isn't a vacation."

"I know you're working. That book is my work as well."

Now I felt like crap because I'd been promising to read it for ages and hadn't done so. I was a terrible friend.

"I'm going to read it. Scout's honor."

"Were you a Girl Scout?"

"No, but I wanted to be one. Does that count?"

"It will have to do," Shelby laughed. "Seriously, do you need to apologize to Dr. Campbell? He's the real deal, Emmy."

I had been…snarky. We'd both said things we probably wish we hadn't. I could say with certainty that we hadn't gotten off on the right foot.

"I will apologize the next time I see him."

"Good, because I've never heard a bad word about him. He's highly respected in all circles and that's saying something."

"I will apologize," I repeated. "I promise. And I'll read your book."

Two promises. Both should be easy to keep.

Why did they feel so difficult?

★ ★ ★

Owen

THE COFFEEMAKER IN my room didn't make the best brew I'd ever tasted but it was adequate. Later I'd go downstairs and have a real breakfast and cup of coffee but it was too early now. The sun was just peeking over the horizon, all orange, blue, and pink.

This was the best time of day as far as I was concerned. I was an unashamed early bird and there was nothing I loved more than a hot cup of coffee while I watched the sun come up. Some mornings I was in too much of hurry but today I was going to sit on my balcony and enjoy it. The minute I'd seen the view from the room overlooking the beach I'd known where I'd be every single morning.

I opened the sliding glass door to the balcony and leaned against the frame to watch the sunrise. It was going to be another glorious day according to the weather service, hot and sunny. Dan and I were planning on doing some snorkeling after breakfast.

Taking a sip of my coffee, I caught something out of the corner of my eye to the right. A flash of blue that wasn't part of the morning sky.

For the love of all that was good and holy. Emmy.

Dressed in a light blue satin nightshirt that just skimmed the tops of her thighs. I had to swallow hard as my gaze ran up and down those perfectly shaped legs. Jesus, she was gorgeous and I was ogling her like a teenage boy. I should stop immediately.

My head, however, wasn't in charge at the moment. Not the one on top of my shoulders, anyway.

Backing away from the doorway slightly I could still see Emmy but I was pretty sure she couldn't see me. Pervert that I was. And am.

A breeze ran through the palm trees and lifted the hem of her nightshirt just a few inches but it was enough for me to witness the gentle curve of her bottom where the creamy skin met the elastic of her panties.

I had to place my hand on my chest to make sure my heart was still beating. I was sure that I'd had a heart attack because my entire body had gone numb for a minute, and now I was sweating despite the mild temperature.

Damn, the tropics are hot as hell.

Emmy had her hands on the railing, leaning over to watch the sunrise, and clearly thought she was alone this early in the morning. I doubted highly that the practical and efficient woman from last night would parade around in her nightie for all and sundry to see. No, she definitely thought she was alone and I was a total asshole for standing here and watching her. A real jerk. I hated myself for it, but not enough to actually move or make my presence known. Another reason I was going to hell. And what was this? A hand basket for my convenience?

As the sun rose in the sky, it cast a pink glow over Emmy's face. She was smiling, her head thrown back and her hair streaming down to the middle of her back, mussed from sleep. She looked happy, content, and at peace. In other words, the exact opposite of every moment she'd spent with me. This was a woman I wanted to know. Not uptight or efficient, but soft, sensual, and reveling in a beautiful sunrise on a Caribbean island.

Could Emerson Grant be more of a romantic than she let on?

Just as quickly as she'd come out on the balcony, she was gone. As soon as the sun had come up and others might have seen her she'd returned to her room, the sound of the door clicking shut firmly behind her. She'd probably get in the shower and get dressed, ready to face the day.

An image of her all steamy and soaped up rose in my consciousness completely unbidden. A rush arousal headed straight to regions below the belt.

Shit. This was bad.

Okay, I was attracted to Emmy but those feelings weren't

returned. At all. She'd made herself clear last night. But I had to admit that she intrigued me. Just who was the real Emmy?

I wasn't ever going to get a chance to find out.

CHAPTER SIX

Emmy

SOMEHOW, I'D MANAGED to avoid Owen most of the day. He'd been busy doing best man stuff and I'd been busy with the last-minute arrangements for the bachelorette party tonight along with the finishing touches for the rehearsal dinner the next evening. But my luck had run out.

Lisa had called me and asked if I would come up to their room. Of course, I said yes and that's how I found myself in their bridal suite along with the happy couple, Owen, and the maid of honor, a lovely woman named Sienna who had an adorable one-year-old girl perched on her hip.

I'd only just arrived and wasn't quite understanding why Lisa was urging Sienna and the little girl to quickly leave the room. Glancing from Owen, to Dan, to Lisa, and back to Owen, I took in their worried expressions but hadn't been able to decipher exactly what was going on.

"I agree with Dan and Lisa," Owen said to Sienna. "You don't want Maddie or yourself to get sick."

Sick? Who was sick?

Sienna looked like she wanted to cry. "I can't just leave you like this."

Like what? Would somebody–

"I don't want you to catch whatever it is that I have," Lisa said, almost in tears as well. "I'd never forgive myself if Maddie got sick."

Ohhhh…I was caught up now. This was so not good in any way shape or form. I'd had sick brides before but it was usually a slight cold or just nerves. Now that I'd taken a really good look at Lisa, I could see that she was pale and her eyes looked glassy. Yes, she was sick alright.

Two days before her wedding. The poor woman.

I was damn good at my job but even I couldn't heal the sick. But a doctor could. I pulled out my phone to call the concierge. There had to a physician on this island and I was going to find him or her and have them in this suite as quickly as humanly possible.

"We'll get a doctor in to see you," I said, pressing the phone to my ear. "Then–"

"You don't need to call a doctor. I know what it is. It's the flu," Lisa broke in, dabbing at her eyes with a tissue. "Everybody at work had it last week. That's why I was working overtime. Now I have it, along with my mom and Dan's brother. That's why Sienna and Maddie shouldn't be here, although it may only be a matter of time before the whole wedding party is sick. We've all been around each other."

All we needed was an epidemic to sweep the resort, turning this happy occasion into disaster of epic proportions. We needed to keep the germs isolated to this wedding party and leave out the other innocent guests. Let's face it…being sick sucked but being sick far from home was even worse. When I'm not feeling well, I want to curl up on my own couch or bed wrapped in my favorite blanket.

"Owen, can you escort Sienna and Maddie out of the suite, please?" I requested, taking charge of the situation. "I'm still going to call a doctor. There are medications that you can take if they catch the flu early enough."

Without any argument Owen did as I asked, gently guiding the mother and child to the door. Dan sat next to Lisa on the couch and rubbed her back in comfort.

"She can't take those medicines, Emmy. She tried a few years ago and she had a bad reaction. Ended up in the hospital. She's going to have to tough this one out. I'll stay with her and make sure she has everything she needs. Lisa's dad is with her mom and my sister-in-law is taking care of my brother."

The concierge answered and I requested a doctor to come to the suite as soon as possible. The minute I said the word *flu*, he sounded pretty motivated.

"Okay," I said, hanging up the phone. "The doctor is coming. I know you said you know what it is and that you can't take anything but I think you should have someone take a look at you anyway. Just in case."

Dan nodded and placed an arm around his bride as they exchanged a glance.

"We're going to have to cancel the wedding," she said softly. "The people at work were sick for days."

That thought had crossed my mind in the last few minutes but I'd tossed it aside in a bout of optimism. With rest and fluids, Lisa might be just fine in forty-eight hours.

"Why don't you wait until the doctor sees you?" I suggested, sitting down on the chair opposite. “Don’t do anything drastic right now.”

The couple exchanged another glance and then Lisa spoke again. “I’d like to speak to Emmy alone please.”

“Babe–”

“No, Dan,” Lisa placed her hand on his and squeezed, a tear falling down her cheek. “I need to talk to Emmy. Why don’t you and Owen step out and get some fresh air? This won’t take long.”

“C’mon, buddy,” Owen said, slapping Dan on the back. “You know better than to argue with a determined woman.”

“I do,” Dan agreed with a weak smile. “We’ll be just outside of you need me. Drink your water, okay?”

Lisa lifted the water bottle from the side table. “I will. I promise. Thank you.”

The two men exited the suite but I could still see them on the balcony. They sat down in the lounge chairs but there was nothing relaxed about their posture.

Lisa took a sip from the water bottle and placed it back on the table. “Emmy, I need you to do something for me.”

“Whatever you need,” I responded instantly. “You name it.”

It was a rash offer but my heart was breaking for this couple I’d grown so fond of. They were lovely people and this entire situation was so unfair. They deserved the wedding of their dreams and right now I was at a loss as to how to give that to them.

“Do you know of any way that Dan and I can get married in the next few hours?” She held up her hand when I opened my mouth to answer. “Please let me finish. Having watched my work colleagues fall to this darn flu one by one I know that I have a short time before this gets really bad. I want to get married, Emmy. I don't need the fancy wedding and the champagne, but I do need this man. I love Dan and I want to be his wife. Is there any way that you can get us married today? I still have enough energy to stand up and say *I do.*"

Tears pricked the back of my eyes at the raw adoration in Lisa's voice. She just wanted to get married to the man she loved. All the trappings were extra. Just the icing on the cake, so to speak.

Glancing up, I could see Dan and Owen standing at the sliding glass door, their noses practically pressed against the glass.

"Will Dan be okay with it?"

Lisa smiled and nodded. "He is. Owen, actually, was the one that suggested it but Dan was on board immediately. I wanted to ask you alone though because I didn't want all three of us to put you under pressure. I know what we're asking may not be possible."

If there was any way in the world I could make this happen, I would. Not because pulling off miracles would be good for my career or business, but because Dan and Lisa deserved it.

"Let me make a few phone calls. I'll do whatever I can to help you."

★ ★ ★

Owen

THIS WAS AN entirely different side of Emerson Grant than she'd showed before. A gentle, tender, caring side that entranced me, making me want to see more. She'd been so sweet with Lisa and Dan, then determined as hell, like a general in the field directing her troops. She'd even drafted me into her army and I'd been happy to help.

With a will of iron, she didn't take no for answer yet found a way to make everyone think it was their idea to pitch in. Before I knew it, she'd put together a wedding ceremony in less than an hour.

Which was why I was standing next to Dan, wearing my tuxedo and grinning like an idiot. We were all smiling, even Lisa, who was paler than only a few hours before but happier than I'd ever seen her.

Not wanting the matron of honor Sienna to get sick and then pass it along to her child, Lisa had asked Emmy to step in and boy, did the wedding planner rise to the occasion. She'd helped Lisa get dressed and then done the bride's hair and makeup. Lisa literally didn't have the strength to apply mascara but Emmy has been there every step of the way despite the fact that she, too, would probably fall ill in a couple of days. Or whatever the incubation period was on this nasty bug. The doctor – who had left about forty-five minutes ago – said that it could be anywhere from two to seven days.

For myself, I had the constitution of an ox and couldn't remember the last time I was sick. I was one of those people with an immune system that worked overtime so I wasn't worried in the least. Even if I hadn't been, there was no way I would have missed this ceremony. Dan was one of my best friends and I'd helped him find Lisa. They were meant for one another and witnessing this was a privilege.

Not wanting to spread any germs to the other guests, the ceremony would take place on the balcony of the suite at sundown. A minister – wearing a mask over his mouth and nose – had been found and was now standing in front of the four of us.

It was time.

"Dearly beloved," he intoned from behind the thin material. "We are gathered here today to join this man and this woman in holy matrimony."

Dan beamed, Lisa's eyes shone with happiness, and I could feel a lump beginning to form in my throat. I couldn't remember a moment in my life where I was as happy as these two were today. And I'd had a fantastic life so far.

Emmy's eyes were shiny with tears as well and I watched as she blinked several times to keep from crying. The practical and efficient planner was far more romantic and sentimental than she admitted to. It only made her more attractive.

She did look absolutely gorgeous, wearing a silky dress that showed off her shoulders. It was a tangerine shade that on anyone else would have looked ridiculous but on her looked exotic and sexy with her golden skin.

"Do you, Daniel, take this woman Lisa to be your wedded wife?"

"I do."

There was no hesitation in Dan's voice. Only emotion and sureness that had me blinking back my own tears.

"And do you, Lisa, take this man Daniel to be your wedding husband?"

"I do."

I could only dream about having a woman look at me the way Lisa was looking at Dan. Emmy sniffled a bit and it wasn't because she was getting sick. She was overcome with the emotion as well.

She had a soft heart. It was tugging at mine.

I needed to get to know this woman much better. Would she let me?

CHAPTER SEVEN

Emmy

DAN HAD PUT Lisa to bed after a short champagne toast where she'd only taken the tiniest sip. I'd thanked the minister and walked him out to the hallway where he'd declined to shake my hand. I didn't take it personally. I was awash in cooties, as was Owen and Dan. If we all didn't end up ill it would be a miracle, although Owen had sworn up and down he never got sick. Dan had backed him in saying his best man had a hearty immune system.

I'd put the specter of impending flu in the back of my mind since I'd found out Lisa and the other wedding guests were sick. Working with people as much as I did, there was always the possibility of getting some nasty crud and ending up in bed drinking tea and watching Netflix for a couple of days. I was of the opinion that I'd been exposed to more germs than the average person and was still standing to tell about it. I'd be fine. I might get sick, I might not, but either way I'd survive in the end.

The ceremony had been beautiful and touching, so loving between Dan and Lisa. They really, honestly loved one another and it had been lovely to witness their vows. I'd been to hundreds of weddings but this one got to me, squeezing at my heart. I'd cried. That wasn't something I did often.

Now that the wedding was over, there were only a few things I need to do tonight. I'd already informed the resort manager that the wedding was cancelled along with the rehearsal dinner and the reception. With guest after guest falling ill, Dan and Lisa had made the difficult decision to cancel all of the events. The healthy guests could enjoy the resort amenities and relax or catch a plane and fly back home. I'd overheard Dan and Owen discussing having a big party in a month or two in our hometown when everyone had recovered.

I needed to make a call to the airlines for myself, but first there was something I needed to do…

Owen had been speaking with Dan before exiting the room to take a phone call. He would be coming back soon so my brief window to apologize was going to quickly close. I needed to get it done.

I slipped out of the sliding glass door to the balcony and stood in the shadows for a moment. Owen was putting his phone back in his pocket, so his call was done. I couldn't put this off any longer.

I stepped out of the shadows and into his path. "Owen, may I have a moment?"

Geez, I sounded uptight. It's just that apologies aren't something I'm all that great at. It always felt liked I'd failed at the situation and I hate failing more than anything in the world.

"Of course, you can. Is everything okay with Lisa?"

"She's fine. Well, as fine as she can be considering the circumstances. She's in bed and drinking some hot tea." I took a deep breath cleansing breath. I might not like apologizing but he deserved it. "I wanted to say that I'm sorry about yesterday. I got snarky about your profession and I apologize."

Hopefully he'd accept it.

For a moment he simply looked at me and I was afraid he was going to tell me to pound sand, but then he smiled. A real one. "It's okay, Emmy. I get where you're coming from and it doesn't bother me. Much. I'm sorry too, by the way."

He laughed and I tried to laugh with him but I still didn't feel good about the situation. He didn't have anything to be sorry about. He hadn't questioned my career choices.

"I really am sorry. My friend pointed out to me that I really don't have an understanding of your work so I should keep my mouth firmly shut, which I plan to do. In fact, I'm going to make that my motto from now on. If I don't know a subject, I need to shut the hell up."

"You're entitled to your opinion, Emmy." He stepped forward, towering over me even in my high heels. He smelled good – again – and my head spun for a second before the earth righted itself. "I think Dan and Lisa would like to be alone. Why don't you let me buy you dinner and maybe I can explain my work a little more? Then you can tell me about yours, of course. It would be only fair."

Dinner? With Owen.

I was tempted. Oh, so tempted. Technically, he wasn't part of the wedding party anymore as the wedding had been cancelled. I'd officially been discharged from work with effusive thanks from the happy couple.

But frankly, I didn't want to start something I couldn't finish. With any luck I'd be home in twelve to eighteen hours.

"I'd like to but I really need to get my return ticket sorted out. I'm hoping to catch a flight out tomorrow."

His smile dimmed slightly. "I didn't realize you were leaving. I'm going to stay the weekend as I'd originally planned."

"I have quite a bit of work waiting for me," I said in way of an explanation. "I hope you don't get sick, too."

Chuckling, he shrugged carelessly. "Seriously, I never get sick. I'll be fine."

There was a moment of silence when neither one of us seemed like we knew what to say.

"I guess I'll go call the airline," I finally said. "Maybe I'll see you in the morning before I leave."

"That would be nice." He walked with me to the door of the suite. "And thank you for the apology. It wasn't necessary but it was sweet."

I couldn't remember the last time anyone had called me sweet. It was kind of nice, but then Owen seemed like a nice man.

The timing sucked. Perhaps if I'd been staying the whole weekend, it might be different. But I wasn't staying, and it wasn't different. The universe was telling me that Dr. Owen Campbell wasn't the man for me. Time to move on.

★ ★ ★

Emmy

"WHAT DO YOU mean there aren't any flights out until Monday morning?"

For the second time, the nice woman on the other end of the

line explained to me that since the island was exclusive and booked for only a few private events this weekend, there would be no service outbound until Monday. Unless it was an emergency of some sort.

"What would constitute an emergency?"

Apparently, she wasn't asked that question often because she hesitated for a moment before answering.

"A heart attack, for example. An injury that the local doctor couldn't take care of."

So, my needing to get home to do a bunch of work didn't qualify.

"You could possibly charter a plane if it's very important," the woman suggested. "I can give you a phone number to call."

Chartering a jet sounded expensive. I wasn't a member of the one percent that frequented resorts like this for fun. I was a hardworking woman who didn't want to blow my retirement account on one flight.

"That's okay. It's probably out of my price range. Thank you for your help."

I hung up and then immediately dialed my friend Shelby to complain about how unfair the world was to me. She answered on the second ring and listened patiently while I told her my tale of woe.

"I'm confused as to how this is a problem," she said when I was done. "Your room is paid for. Your flight is paid for. Girl, it's time for a vacation. Party down or whatever it is they say. Have some fun. Drink an umbrella drink and get a tan. You're acting like this is a tragedy when this is the greatest thing that's happened to you in a long while."

"I have so much work–"

"That will be there when you get home," Shelby replied before I could finish. "You weren't planning on doing that work until Tuesday and you were fine with it. Besides, your assistants can handle things when you're away, right?"

I'd just hired my third assistant and they were all amazing. I'd lucked out. They were awesome and then some.

"They're great," I agreed. "But there are some things I need to do myself."

"And you can," Shelby agreed cheerfully. "On Tuesday when you get back to the office. In the meantime, have fun. Speaking of fun, did you apologize to Dr. Campbell?"

"I did and he accepted it gracefully." I paused, not sure I should even open this can of worms. "I don't think he was upset with me. He asked me to have dinner with him tonight."

"What did you say?" Shelby demanded. "Did you say yes?"

"I said no because I needed to make arrangements to go home."

"Then call him and tell him you're not leaving. Put me on hold."

"I am not going to call him and tell him that I've changed my mind. He could have one of the cocktail waitresses as a date by now."

Although he hadn't really seemed like the horn dog type.

"I still think you should call him."

"So noted."

"If you aren't going to have dinner with him then you have lots of free time this weekend to read my book."

Laughing at my friend's persistence, I could only agree. "I

should have tons of time. I have it with me so I'll get back to it tonight. I'll probably just order up some room service for dinner."

"You should go dancing. Have some fun. When was the last time you had some wild fun?"

I knew exactly when.

"Ashlyn's birthday party. We all took turns puking the next morning."

"It was all Ashlyn's fault," Shelby replied. "She was the first to throw up. I wouldn't have puked but she started in and I couldn't control it after that."

My story was pretty much the same.

"It was everyone's fault because we know better than to mix grape and grain."

"Go out and have too much rum tonight. Meet a mysterious man and have wild sex on the beach."

Sometimes Shelby baffled me.

"In no way, shape, or form can I see that happening. Have I ever given you any indication in the least that I longed to do that?"

"No, but you should. You are far too buttoned up most of the time. Let your hair down. Have some fun. What happens on the island, stays on the island."

"People say that but it's never true. And I am not too *buttoned up*. I can cut loose with the best of them."

"You can but you don't very often. Now you have the chance. Go for it. You know you want to."

Did I want to? In a way I did. Because I had to be in control and in charge all the time cutting loose wasn't an activity that I engaged in often. Yes, I had had a few too many drinks at Ashlyn's party but we hadn't done anything crazy like go out to a pasture and tip cows or anything.

"I'll think about it, Shel. Now tell me how your day is going."

Let's face it. I just wasn't the spontaneous, go for it type. I'd spend the evening reading and watching television.

Just like every other night.

CHAPTER EIGHT

Owen

I'D THOUGHT ABOUT having dinner in my room but I was too restless to stare at the four walls and docilely eat my meal. I didn't have an issue eating dinner alone in the restaurant, which was good since Emmy had turned me down when I'd asked her to join me. Her excuse hadn't been the greatest but I hadn't pressed her on the invitation.

Honestly, she'd looked exhausted, dark circles beginning to show under her eyes. All the work of putting together the last-minute wedding ceremony had fallen to her and if she was tired, she had a damn good reason to be. She might also not want to spend any more time with a wedding party that was clearly cursed with the plague. Or something close to it. I assumed she was going to order room service and get some well-deserved rest before her flight tomorrow.

Because she was leaving. A fact that didn't make me all that happy but I was determined to give her a call when I returned home. Emmy Grant was far too fascinating to ignore. I wanted to get to know her and find out if she was as amazing as she appeared to be.

So I was surprised to see her exiting the kitchen of the casual restaurant at the back of the resort. I was standing at the entrance waiting to be seated and she was going to have to walk right by me.

"Emmy, I didn't expect to see you here."

Since you turned me down for dinner. My ego was a little bruised.

"I was checking with the chef about the cancelled meals and the wedding cake. He's going to try and save it for a few days in case Lisa and Dan feel better and might want some of it. I hated to see it go to waste after all the time they spent picking it out."

"Lemon curd."

Her brows pinched together in confusion.

"Pardon?"

"Lemon curd," I repeated with a grin. "Lisa went on and on about how she'd chosen lemon curd as one of the fillings along with a peppermint white chocolate, and dark chocolate ganache."

"Goodness, you have an excellent memory."

"What can I say? I was really looking forward to that cake. I have a sweet tooth."

Biting her lip, Emmy leaned forward so only I could hear what she was about to say. I caught a whiff of her perfume – mixture of vanilla and coconut. Maybe some musk, too. Let's face it, I didn't know shit about women's fragrances. I only knew if I liked them.

I loved this one.

"Then I can admit to you that I was looking forward to it, too," Emmy sighed. "Especially the dark chocolate ganache."

What the hell. The worst thing she could do is call the cops and accuse me of stalking.

"I'm told they have good desserts here. I don't suppose I can convince you to take pity and join me for dinner? I promise if you say no, I won't make a pest of myself and keep asking."

Indecision flickered over her features, her top teeth sinking even deeper into her full lower lip. I was sure she was going to turn me down. Again.

"Thank you. I'd love to join you for dinner."

I didn't expect that. But I wasn't going to question my good luck too much. Just enjoy it.

The hovering hostess quickly seated us in a quiet corner that overlooked the pool and garden area, placing a menu in front of each of us.

"Did you get your plane reservation made?"

"That's a good question." Emmy sighed and placed her menu on the table. "I tried but it turns out the one little airline that services this island isn't planning any flights out until Monday morning. So…I guess you could say that I'm on vacation starting now."

Emmy wasn't leaving. She was staying. Cue the happy music and fireworks. This just might be my lucky day. The universe was on my side.

"You don't sound as happy about that as one might expect you to."

She wrinkled her nose and checked out the menu again. "It's just that I had a ton of work back at home. But my friends are urging me to take the opportunity to relax and have fun. Shelby told me to drink too much rum tonight and do something…wild."

I could help her with that.

"Too much rum and wildness? That sounds pretty exciting. Are you going to do it?"

Please say yes, please say yes.

Emmy just laughed. "I might drink some rum but do something wild? It's not really in my nature. I'm a cautious person."

Damn.

I signaled the waitress. "Let me help you get started by ordering us two rum drinks. Then you can tell me about your friend Shelby. She sounds like quite the character."

"She is. She's a psychologist as well and she knows you. Dr. Shelby Kelly?"

His face lit up with delight. "That Shelby? She's fantastic. I haven't seen her in months. How is she doing?"

Finally. We had a subject we could talk about. Things were looking up.

★ ★ ★

Emmy

"I'M AN ONLY child," Owen said over our delicious entrees when I'd asked about his family. I'd ordered the rosemary chicken and he was digging into a filet – medium rare. "I always wanted brothers and sisters but it wasn't to be. I never even had a pet. But I did have an entire bathroom to myself. I guess that's one good thing."

"You don't know what it's like for three teenage girls to try and do their hair and makeup all at the same time. It's a recipe for disaster. There wasn't anything else good about being an only child? You didn't have to share anything. That must have been nice."

He seemed to ponder my question longer than usual. "It was, although I would have gladly shared my room or my toys. I was lonely growing up. Let's just say that I talked to my stuffed animals way more than I probably should have."

That was so incredibly sad.

Taking a sip of my wine, I wasn't sure what to say. Was I bringing up bad memories? Did I need to change the subject?

"I'm sorry. That must have been terrible."

"I wouldn't say it was terrible but my upbringing was far different than most people."

"How so?" The question jumped out of my mouth before I could stop it. "I'm sorry. That was nosy. Please ignore me."

He shook his head. "I wouldn't have brought it up if I wasn't okay talking about it. I had a weird childhood, but it shaped me into who I am so I can't regret it. In telling the story I would have to start with my parents. They should never have had a child. In fact, I'm firmly convinced that I was an unplanned mistake, although to their credit they never said that to me. They simply weren't the type who had strong maternal or paternal feelings. They didn't know or want to know how to parent."

How awful. Utterly sad.

"So you raised yourself?"

Chuckling, he shook his head. "I was raised by a series of nannies until I was sixteen. At that age my parents considered me an adult and proceeded to treat me that way."

"Were you?" I asked, completely intrigued by his story, so different than my own boring as hell childhood. "An adult, I mean?"

His smile widened and his chuckle turned into a laugh. "Not by a longshot. I did so much stupid shit in high school. I really should be dead. My parents didn't know about most of it and I doubt they would have cared either way. They would have said that I was testing my boundaries or something."

"What kind of stuff did you do?"

"I didn't have a curfew so I'd stay out all night."

"Didn't your friends have curfews?"

He nodded and grinned. "They did. So after midnight I was hanging out with guys who were older than me. We were definitely up to no good. Drinking and partying."

"And no one knew that you were only sixteen?"

"I was big for my age."

I was...surprised. The mature man sitting across from me was so different than what he was describing.

"I'll admit that I'm having trouble picturing you as a juvenile delinquent. And your parents never found out?"

"Nope, and they wouldn't have cared. Like I said, they simply should never have had a child. They were too engrossed in their own lives."

"What did your parents do?"

"They were archeologists. They were gone a lot."

The picture was becoming much clearer.

"And they left you behind with a nanny?"

"Yes, but don't feel sorry for me, Emmy. I'm not scarred for life or anything. But it did help me decide what I wanted to be when I grew up."

"A psychologist?"

He nodded. "Yes, although I started out researching child and parent relationships but quickly found that romantic relationships were far more fascinating. Or maybe I just didn't want to dig into my own family dynamic? Either way, I don't regret anything. We're all a product of our upbringing to a certain extent. It's what we do with it that's important."

"Are you close to your parents now?"

"No, Emmy. I'm not." His tone was gentle but firm. "Thankfully, we've given up any pretense of being a family. The last time I saw them was…about four years ago at a cousin's wedding."

I couldn't imagine not having any family. I complained about mine but in the end, I loved them to death.

"I would think they'd be proud of you and your achievements," I muttered, shoving a forkful of potatoes in my mouth. Owen, on the other hand, appeared completely unperturbed by his parents' cold attitudes.

"They're good people, Emmy. They just never should have been parents."

I wanted to slap my fork down on the plate. Loudly. "You shouldn't defend them. They don't deserve it. They may not have wanted to be parents, Owen, but by God they brought you into this world. You deserve to have parents who give a shit. It's not fair."

"Life isn't fair."

"You're far too forgiving."

If I ever met his mother and father, I'm not sure that I wouldn't be able to keep from smacking them upside their heads. Or maybe stomping on their toes.

"Did you ever think that I forgave them for myself, not for them?"

"Well…no. Dammit…"

"You're a sweet woman, Emmy Grant. You want to make everything okay for me even though it's been years since I was a child. I'm a psychologist. Believe me, I've worked through the anger and come to this place of acceptance. I can't change the past and I can't change my parents. There was a time in my life when I thought I could and it brought me nothing but heartache and frustration. But you are right…I deserve better. That's why I don't bother to try and have them in my life anymore."

"That's very mentally healthy."

"It took a long time to get there. But I think it explains why I'm so passionate about creating love and happiness, and why I want it for myself."

My mouth went dry and I took a quick gulp from my water glass. Most men wouldn't have said that out loud.

"You want to get…married?"

Consider me stunned. I was probably staring at him like a deer in headlights.

"Absolutely. Marriage, kids, a dog. The whole nine yards. I just haven't found the right person yet, but I'm looking."

He was looking. Actively. Because he wanted to get married and have a family.

I couldn't remember the last time a man had said those words to me. Years?

Don't get me wrong. I was aware there were plenty of men that wanted to settle down with the right woman; it's just that I hadn't dated any of them in a long time. Not that I was on a date with Owen. Or was I? Was this a date? Holy shit. I might be on a date with Owen.

That was more disturbing than hearing he wanted to get married.

Clearing my throat, I took another big drink of my water. Suddenly I was really thirsty.

"In your job you must be exposed to millions of eligible women."

That brought me down to earth with a hard thunk. Millions of women. Prettier. Smarter. Funnier. Sexier. Less neurotic.

His brows pinched together and he rubbed his chin. There was just a bit of stubble there.

"In a way, although I don't make a habit of fishing off the company pier, so to speak. I have, of course, taken my own test and I do look for matches but I haven't found anyone I've been interested in, to be honest."

He was looking at me. Like *really* looking at me. As if he was trying to see inside me all the way to my soul. Was he saying that he was interested? If he was, what did I think about that?

I think I liked the idea. If he was interested.

Why couldn't men have a sign that popped up over their heads when they found a woman attractive? It would make life so much easier. I was decent with body language but I couldn't quite get a read on Owen except that he was relaxed and open with me. I didn't get any subterfuge from him, no bragging or preening. He was...himself.

How novel.

"What about you, Emmy? Are you close to your family?"

It appeared we were done with the marriage and commitment portion of the evening. Thank goodness. It was stressful as hell.

CHAPTER NINE

Owen

EMMY LOVED HER family. It was easy to see as she lit up when talking about her brother and two sisters, plus her parents. Her expression would go all soft when she described her mom and dad. Earlier in the evening, she'd talked a little about her childhood but then she'd changed the subject to me. I wanted to know more about *her*.

"Were you the middle child?"

Shit. I needed to keep my damn mouth shut, but sometimes the doctor in me came spilling out.

Frowning, she tilted her head at my question. "Yes. How did you know?"

Fuck. Because I was a psychologist and it was obvious. Women, however, didn't necessarily find that fun and attractive on a date.

Wait…was this a date? I'd asked her to have dinner with me. I wanted it to be a date. I wanted to kiss her at the end of the evening. Or earlier, if that could be arranged. Did she think this was some casual meal that two acquaintances were sharing? Shit.

"A lucky guess, that's all."

Her eyes narrowed and she made a huffing sound. "Because

I'm efficient and practical and don't like to be the center of attention?"

Among other reasons.

An alarm went off in my head. *Danger. Divert. Change the subject and fast.*

"Would you like dessert?"

Shaking her head, she placed her napkin on the table. "I'm stuffed. There's no way I could eat another bite. It was so good, though."

The meal had been wonderful. This resort had earned its reputation.

"How about a walk on the beach?" I suggested. "It's a beautiful night."

I held my breath as she contemplated my offer. If she said yes, then we both definitely knew it was a date. If she said no, then it was still up in the air. She might know it was a date but not be enjoying it, or she didn't know it was a date and my question sounded creepy.

"I'd like that." She leaned forward, a brow raised. "But don't think I don't know what you're doing. I know you're trying to get my mind off of your statement that I'm the middle child."

I almost choked on my drink. "Why would I do that?"

"For obvious reasons. And I'm going to let you. For now. How about that walk?"

"I'll get the check and we'll go."

Moonlight, a warm breeze, sand beneath our feet, and the sound of the tide. It was a recipe for romance and this woman made me feel very romantic indeed. I wanted to kiss her under the stars.

★ ★ ★

Emmy

IF ANYONE HAD told me a few days ago that I would be strolling down a moonlit beach, my shoes in one hand and the other held by a gorgeous man, I would have told them they were insane. I wouldn't have time for fun and romance. But here I was and this was most definitely romantic.

I was a practical woman, but even I wasn't immune to the sound of the waves against the sand and the stars hanging overhead. Palm trees swayed in the gentle breeze and the smell of salt and coconut oil was in the air. The entire scene was pure seduction. It didn't help that I might have had a little too much rum at dinner, but the drinks were so delicious. A rum drink at home simply didn't taste the same way it did in the tropics.

"You're very quiet," Owen said, his fingers entwined with mine. It felt good. "Was it something I said?"

"No. I'm just enjoying the serenity."

"Then do you want me to shut up?"

Laughing, I shook my head. He was a good sport and had a nice sense of humor. "Not at all. I like talking to you. You don't ramble on and on about sports."

"You don't like sports?"

"I like sports just fine but I don't want them to be my sole focus of conversation and life in general. There are other topics that are interesting, too."

Geez, I sounded uptight. Again. Maybe I needed this vacation more than I thought. Time to relax.

"Such as?"

"Movies. Books. Music. Food. Those are just a few."

Somehow, we'd stopped walking and were standing just on the edge of the water. If I took just one tiny step to the left the waves would have lapped at my bare toes.

The moon shone down brightly and I could see Owen's far too handsome face. He was wearing a playful smile.

"Okay, this sounds like fun. What's your favorite movie?"

We were going to play a game? Why not? Shelby was constantly telling me I needed to lighten up and have some fun.

"*Mary Poppins.*"

His shoulders shook with laughter. At me.

"*Mary Poppins?* I can see why."

"She's practically perfect in every way," I replied tartly, knowing full well why he was laughing. "And Dick Van Dyke is terrific. But it's the music that steals the movie."

"It is a great film. I'm not arguing."

"What's your favorite movie?"

"*Citizen Kane.*"

"I saw that once. It was good."

"But no dancing penguins."

"It would have been improved by a big musical number at the end."

In fact, I think most films could be improved that way.

"I agree. I don't know why Orson Welles didn't include one. How about food? What's your favorite food? Mine is spaghetti and meatballs."

I liked Owen when he was like this. A bit silly and fun. I didn't care if he laughed at me a little because he would be fine with me laughing at him.

He was becoming more attractive by the minute. I was in dangerous territory.

"Spaghetti sounds really good but I think my favorite is fried chicken. I know it's bad for me though, so I don't eat it too often."

His fingers slid up the flesh of my arm, leaving a trail of tingles in their wake. "I eat spaghetti at least once a week."

He moved a step closer so that our bodies were almost touching. Not quite but almost. My breath caught and my knees turned to jelly.

"Can you cook?"

"I can. One of my nannies taught me. You name it and I can probably make it."

Leaning down, his gaze captured mine. I could feel the heat from his body and feel his warm breath on my cheek. Shit. Butterflies danced in my stomach and my heart had crawled up into my throat making it difficult to talk. I was able to get out one single word.

"Meatloaf."

I sounded like Kermit the Frog.

"Yes."

"Pizza."

"Who makes pizza? I order it in. But I probably could make it if I tried. It's just a bit of dough, sauce, and cheese."

I couldn't seem to look away and the tension between us grew into a palpable thing. I wanted him to kiss me. I think he wanted to as well. The idea of simply throwing myself into his arms crossed my mind but the still sane part of my brain kept me standing firmly in the same spot.

Okay, maybe I wasn't all that sane. It could just be sheer fear of rejection. What if I was imagining all of this?

"Coq au vin."

Kiss me.

"You got me. That's one I can't do."

Who cares? Kiss me. Just grab me and do it. I think you want to. I know I want you to.

"Emmy? Are you okay?"

No, I'm not. For the first time in months, maybe even a year, I'm with a man I'm truly attracted to.

"I don't care that you like the outdoors."

Fuck. What in the hell was I saying? I'm babbling like a fool. I glanced down at the sand trying to calculate how much time and effort it would take to dig a hole and disappear. I could feel the heat in my cheeks and I hoped it would continue because then I could just melt away into a pile of goo.

If Owen thought my statement was strange, he was too polite to say so. He smiled and his fingers came up under my chin, his thumb caressing my sensitive skin. I couldn't stop the shiver that ran through me and dammit, he noticed, of course. Even in the moonlight I could see his expression of triumph.

Just kiss me.

"I don't care that you don't like the outdoors, Emmy."

Owen didn't make me wait any longer. Bending his head, his lips captured my own, tentatively at first and then more powerfully when I didn't back away or slap his face. He had one hand cupped behind my head as if he was afraid I was going to twist away, but that definitely wasn't going to happen. This man knew how to kiss.

Not too wet. Not too dry. Just the right amount of pressure. Then he softly ran his tongue over my lower lip and I opened up to him as he pulled me closer. Pressed up against his hard chest, I could feel his heart beat and smell the tang of his body wash, clean and crisp. It filled my nostrils and made me dizzy, or it could have been the kiss.

It was probably the kiss.

I don't know how long we might have stood there, lost in each other but the sound of people approaching had us pulling apart. I wasn't one for public displays and this beach wasn't exactly private.

Our breathing was ragged as we stood there, staring at one another. I didn't know what to say and I never did at a moment like this. Did we high five? Did I compliment his kissing prowess?

I should have read the chapter in Shelby's book that talked about the first kiss. Too late now.

I didn't come to this island for a vacation romance. Heck, I didn't even come here for a vacation, but I was smacked dab in the middle of one and I wasn't sorry.

I liked Owen Campbell, and I was going to have some damn fun while I had the chance.

Even though it wasn't practical in the least.

★ ★ ★

AFTER DROPPING EMMY at her hotel room door – with another

kiss – I walked the three feet to my own room and went inside. The evening had turned out much differently than I'd expected it to. It had been a surprise to see Emmy in the restaurant and an even bigger shock that she'd agreed to dine with me. The most important fact, however, was…

I was blown away by the kiss. Just knocked on my ass and left for dead.

What an amazing woman and what a fan – fucking – tastic kiss.

She might not like the outdoors and she thought *Citizen Kane* should be a musical. She was adorable and I was falling fast and hard. Emmy Grant was a delicious combination of efficient, practical, fanciful, and fun with a side of hotter than sin. My lips were still on fire from that kiss. She ought to be illegal in all fifty states, or at the very least come with a warning label.

Clearly, all the men she'd dated in the past were idiots to let her slip through their fingers. Luckily, I was no dummy. I couldn't wait to spend more time getting to know her. I'd made sure to make a date for the next day.

I wanted to make it special. A woman like Emmy, who planned events for a living, wasn't going to be easy to impress.

What could we do to make it a memorable day?

★ ★ ★

AFTER QUICKLY SHOWERING and brushing my teeth, I slipped into an old t-shirt and under the covers. I'd promised to work on reading Shelby's book but honestly that wasn't why I was retrieving it from my carryon bag.

I needed to figure out what in the hell I was doing with Owen.

I wasn't a virgin. I'd dated lots of men over the years, some I'd slept with and some that I didn't. I liked sex and didn't have any guilt about engaging in it. I was human and humans are sexual beings. We like pleasure and sex – with the right guy – was pleasurable. When I was between boyfriends, I also had a vibrator in my bedside table. It sat next to a small bottle of lubricant and a box of condoms.

Because one never knows. I wanted to be prepared.

I'd even had a few one-night stands when I was younger. I wasn't exactly proud of that but I wasn't ashamed, either. I considered it part of being young and dumb. It wasn't an activity I was planning on doing now.

I say all of this so you'll understand that I'm no novice in the dating, romance, and sex department. In fact, I considered myself to be fairly savvy when it came to men. But there was something about Owen that turned me into a gawky teenager. I hadn't even been one of those when I *was* a teenager.

When he'd touched me I could barely talk, and when he'd kissed me I went all weak in the knees. My heart had pounded and my palms had covered in sweat. I don't remember ever being this nervous… At least not as a grown ass adult. Wait. I'd been pretty beside myself the day I'd signed the mortgage papers to my townhouse but that had been a thirty-year commitment. A person should be nervous, I think, when signing their life away.

Hopefully, Shelby's book had some answers because I had more than a few questions. I skipped the *finding a man* part that

I had been skimming and went straight to the *dating* section.

Chapter Six. Don't be too into him until he's into you.

Words to live by.

I settled back onto a stack of pillows, ready to plow through several chapters. I needed some wisdom and I needed it now.

Owen Campbell could be dangerous for my equilibrium.

CHAPTER TEN

Emmy

I HAD A date with Owen this morning, and by the way I was acting, an innocent bystander might think it was my first date ever in my entire life. I was as giddy as a schoolgirl, changing my clothes several times and doing my hair in different styles until I finally settled on a simple ponytail.

The outfit, however, was still up in the air.

He'd mentioned spending time on the beach but he'd also said that we would have lunch, too. With that sketchy information I was currently wearing shorts and a tank top over my swimsuit but five minutes ago I'd been wearing a sundress and before that capris and a striped cotton shirt.

Damn. I stripped off the tank top, tossing it on the bed, and replaced it with the cotton shirt. Much better.

I'd been awake until after midnight reading Shelby's "trap a man" book. If this was how Shelby acted in her dating life before she was engaged, then I was officially impressed. She'd been a total bad ass. A take no prisoners, suffer no fools female that kicked ass and didn't bother to take any names later. She took chances in a bold and courageous way that I could only admire.

The advice that had stuck with me was that I needed to take

my time when entering into any sort of relationship. Don't rush it. Savor the journey. Enjoy the romance. Revel in the act of getting to know a person.

That's what I was going to do. Savor. Enjoy. Too often when I'd dated in the past, I'd been sizing up a guy on the first date as to whether he was the kind of person I could have any sort of future with. Shelby said that was a common mistake and it created complications where there didn't need to be any, especially as women get to be thirty and over. We think that we should only be dating "appropriate" men.

Believe me, I never cared about that when I was younger. When had it all changed?

A knock on the door had me shoving my feet into a pair of flip flops and throwing my beach bag over my shoulder. One last look in the mirror told me that my lip balm was still shiny and pink right along with my cheeks.

I opened the door and was once again reminded just how good-looking Owen was. Today he was wearing a faded pair of cargo shorts and a forest green t-shirt that molded to his muscled chest and flat abs. Yummy.

"Hi."

That's right. I'm a grown woman, respected in my field, and when confronted with a sexy male I suddenly cannot form two-word sentences. Actually, it was only with *this* particular male animal. I usually had it pretty together with everyone else.

"Hi, you look lovely. Are you ready to go?"

"Thank you, and yes, I'm ready to go."

Although I didn't know exactly where we were heading.

He slipped his hand into mine, tangling our fingers together as he led me out of the hotel. The day was perfect for the beach, and I could feel the warmth of the sun on my skin and smell the salt in the air. What was the temperature back home?

Cold as hell.

"Where are we going?" I asked when we didn't take the path to the beach.

"I can tell you or you can be surprised," he replied with a grin. "I don't know you well enough to know if you even like surprises. Many people don't. It's up to you."

A surprise. Shelby hated them and Ashlyn wasn't too fond of them, either. Mia loved them. What about me? Hmmm…

I think that I liked them. For the most part. Of course, I'd had a few that really sucked but what were the chances today? Owen wasn't going to take me somewhere that he thought was unpleasant.

Relax. Savor. Enjoy. Don't have an agenda.

"Surprise me."

His expression lit up like a little kid. "That's great. Just follow me."

I did follow him all the way to a marina – about a ten-minute walk – that I didn't know existed on this island and I thought I'd known everything about this resort. Stopping beside a shiny boat with red stripes, Owen held out his hand to me.

"Are you ready to take a little ride?"

"I think I'd love that." I let him help me over the side of the small craft and into the bow section where there were seats. We weren't alone, however. There was a captain manning the wheel. "Thank you."

Owen settled into the seat next to me, his arm around my

shoulders. "You are welcome. Now Hal here is going to drive and all we have to do is sit back and enjoy the ride."

The engine growled and then roared to life, vibrating under our seat. The boat might not be large but it was clearly powerful. A fact that became evident when we exited the no wake zone and were in open water. This would be no leisurely meandering to our destination. Hal was driving the hell out of this boat.

I loved it.

The rush of wind on my cheeks, lifting my ponytail straight up into the air. The intermittent spray of water that came over the side, landing cool droplets on my skin. My heart raced along with my adrenaline as the boat sliced cleanly through the waves. Where we were going didn't matter in the least. For the first time in a long time, I was simply loving the journey which was over far too soon.

Before I knew it, we were pulling up to a deserted strip of beach, the boat bobbing with the tide as Owen lifted me over the side. The captain handed him a large cooler with a blanket on the top and we walked through the surf to the dry sand.

Hal tapped his watch. "Two o'clock. I'll be back. Have fun."

With another growl of the engine he zipped away, leaving me and Owen. All alone. Despite the heat, a shiver ran up my spine.

"Where are we?"

A nice neutral question when what I really wanted to ask him was what he had in mind bringing me here.

"A tiny little island a few miles from the main. It's owned by the resort and they plan to develop it eventually with bungalows but right now it's deserted." Owen lifted up the blanket. "How about we spread this out?"

"How did you know about this? I didn't know."

"I only knew because I specifically asked the concierge last night about a quiet location to have a picnic. She suggested this place."

"No one said anything to me when I was discussing wedding and reception venues."

"Maybe I was more charming?"

Snorting, I reached for the blanket, spreading out my two corners while he did his side. We settled on top of it and I shrugged off my shirt and shorts, anxious to get into the water and cool off. I'd worn a sapphire blue two piece under my clothes that was actually rather modest but I suddenly felt way too naked. Owen, to his credit, wasn't staring at me or being creepy but I could feel his gaze like a physical caress as it swept me from head to toe.

I wanted him to like what he saw. Because I sure as hell was enjoying what I was looking at.

Owen had stood and slipped his cargo shorts down his legs before tugging his t-shirt over his head, revealing a deliciously muscular torso with ridged abs. I had a sudden urge to run my tongue over them one by one.

Hey, I was supposed to be savoring this, right? Was it wrong to admire the male form? Was I objectifying him? That would be wrong, but I couldn't seem to rip my gaze from his well-formed physique.

"Did you want to go for a swim?"

He'd asked me a question and now I had to make my mouth form words.

"Yes." Okay, one word. I could do better, though. "I need to put on some sunscreen first."

I hadn't completely lost my common sense. I didn't want to turn into a sunburned mess. Digging into my bag, I pulled out a bottle of sunscreen, keeping my eyes trained on the blanket. Anywhere but on him. Giving myself a mental smack in the forehead, I smeared some of the white cream into my arms, legs, and chest. I was about to tuck the bottle away when I felt him sitting behind me, his hand held out. For what?

"We don't want you to burn. Why don't you let me put some of that on your back?"

Yes, please. I couldn't lie to myself. I'd kind of been hoping he would offer to do it.

"Thank you."

My voice sounded huskier than normal but not high or squeaky, which was an accomplishment considering how quivery I was on the inside. My stomach was tied and twisted into a series of intricate knots that would have earned a Boy Scout his badge. Holding my breath, I waited for the first touch of his fingers.

Heat. That was my first impression. His digits left a trail of warmth everywhere he touched. Long magical strokes, first on my shoulders and then slowly and deliberately down my spine until I was drifting on a cloud, ignoring the world and reality. So it was a sharp drop to earth when he pulled his hands away.

"That should keep you from burning."

The practical side of me should have been thrilled. No sunburns. At the moment, I didn't give a rat's ass about skin cancer or wrinkles. My brain was taken up with steamy images of Owen and I making out on the beach…

Like the couple in that old black and white movie *From Here to Eternity*. I'd watched it one night with Shelby, Ashlyn, and Mia while we ate pizza and drank too much wine. They'd all thought it was incredibly romantic but I, of course, had questioned whether their ass cracks would be full of sand the next day. I stand by that too, but this man might just be worth it.

"Thank you."

I accepted the bottle from him but didn't put it back into my bag, my mind already working on those images.

"What about you? Do you need some sunscreen?"

To my disappointment, he shook his head. "I guess I was just born lucky because I never burn. Ready to take a swim?"

As if I could even stand on my Jell-O knees. But I accepted his hand up and we walked to the edge, letting the waves lap at our feet. The water was cold in contrast to the hot sun and that gave me an idea. A really awful, terrible, but wonderful idea. Owen had been such a good sport up to now, and I desperately needed to break the tension that had built up at his first touch.

Without alerting him to my diabolic plan, I brought my foot back and kicked out hard, sending a spray of water in Owen's direction. Success.

It landed on his leg and he looked shocked for a moment but then he gave an evil laugh and waggled his brows. Shit, I was in trouble. Reaching down with those gigantic hands into the pool at our feet, he tossed that cold water back at me, hitting me square in the stomach. Squealing, I danced around in the surf indignantly but I'd taken the first shot in the battle and now it was war.

Game on.

We played for a little while, splashing and chasing each other in the surf, and acting like a couple of kids. By the time I gave up – that's right, I surrendered first – we were both soaked but laughing so hard our ribs hurt. At least mine did, and he was holding his side so I assumed he felt the same.

"Okay, you won," I said again, panting and giggling while trying to drag oxygen into my aching lungs. I'd fallen to my knees in pure exhaustion. "I give up."

"You started this," Owen replied, kneeling down next to me, his own chest rising and falling rapidly. At least I wasn't the only person sucking wind. "Did you actually think you'd win? I run five miles a day."

"I do yoga," I gasped, my hands braced on my thighs. "That's exercise."

"Yoga?" Owen didn't sound impressed. "Does that help your endurance?"

It probably would if I went to class with any regularity. Lifting my head to reply to his question, I was instead caught up in his heated gaze. Our eyes locked and suddenly I wasn't laughing anymore. That tension that I sought desperately to dispel was back but this time on steroids. I could feel the heat from Owen's body, far hotter than the sun overhead, and see the desire in his eyes that he didn't bother to hide. It ratcheted up my own arousal to be so blatantly wanted.

Passion zipped through my veins and the blood roared in my ears like a freight train. We were all alone and already half naked. It didn't take much for our imaginations to take it the rest of the way.

We fell into each other's arms, our lips crashing together. I don't know which one of us moved first but it didn't really matter. We were both enthusiastic participants in the current activity.

Linking my arms around his neck, I pulled him closer, trailing my lips along his stubbly jaw before running my tongue right at the spot below his ear. His skin had the tang of salt and sweat.

Owen gave a purely masculine growl and the next thing I knew I was flat on my back in the sand, his large frame hovering above me. Bending his head, he dropped baby kisses all over my face, as soft as the fluttering of butterfly wings. It was such a dichotomy – this powerful man ever so tender and gentle.

My nails dug into the muscles of his shoulders as his lips traveled down my neck to the spot where my pulse beat madly. He nipped at the skin and then soothed it with his tongue, drawing lazy circles in a path down to the curve of my breast before creating a damp trail straight to my belly button. My torso arched up off of the sand and my eyes drifted closed as he pressed openmouthed kisses to my abdomen.

If this was a dream, I never wanted to wake up.

★ ★ ★

WE NEEDED TO slow the hell down before we did something that Emmy might regret afterward. I sure as hell wouldn't be sorry but I couldn't stand to see it in her eyes if we rushed into a physical relationship too quickly. On a sandy beach, no less.

It might look incredibly romantic like in a movie, but I'd been down this road before and was left with a butt crack full of sand. I wanted far more for my first time with Emmy. Some soft music, low lights, good food, and a damn comfortable mattress.

Easing away, I pressed one last kiss to her swollen lips before resting back on my heels. Stretched out beneath me she was gorgeous as hell and my cock was painfully protesting my chivalry. I was hard and ready but at my age I wasn't under the false delusion that I was going to perish from a case of blue balls. I was mighty uncomfortable and I had the sudden urge to dive straight into the cool water.

Later, Romeo.

"I think we should slow down, honey."

Her lips fluttered open at my words and at first she didn't say anything, but then she slowly nodded in agreement. She sat up and brushed the sand from her legs, a futile task. We were covered in it.

"I guess you're right."

I had assumed she'd sound relieved, but no. She actually sounded perturbed. Was she angry that I'd stopped? I was trying to be a fucking gentleman, dammit.

That's when I tried to explain.

"I didn't want you to regret anything later," I said, my words coming out in a rush. "I wanted us both to be sure."

"Yes, I agree."

That's what her words said, but her expression didn't match. She looked angry and I opened my mouth to confront her about it, but then it occurred to my addled brain what was going on. I snapped my mouth shut and jumped to my feet, holding out a hand to help her up.

Emmy wasn't angry. She was frustrated. In a sexual sense. We both were and it didn't do anything to enhance our moods. Her mind might agree that we needed to slow down but her body hadn't received the message yet.

One glance down told me that my body also hadn't gotten the memo. If she pushed me down into the sand and mounted me, I'd be as ready as I'd ever been in my life.

Cold water was the only answer.

"We should rinse off this sand," I suggested. "We don't want it to get on the blanket. Are you getting hungry? I had the resort pack us a lunch in the cooler."

Maybe if we concentrated on food, we'd forget about sex.

I know…not likely, but it was worth a shot.

"That sounds good," she replied. "Food, I mean."

It was going to be a long afternoon. Why did I stop again?

CHAPTER ELEVEN

Emmy

I'D MADE A fool of myself this afternoon and I was of two minds about spending the evening with Owen. I'd agreed to have a casual dinner with him in his suite and then watch a movie, but after my behavior on the beach earlier I wasn't sure that I could face him.

Mortified. That's what I was.

Because while Owen had been pretty calm, cool, and collected about stopping our tryst midway I'd been much less on board with it. In fact, I'd been rather miffed about the whole situation.

He certainly knew his way around a woman, and he'd known what to do to get my motor revving. I'd been primed and ready for more when he'd abruptly put the brakes on. *Coitus interruptus* makes me cranky.

There. I'd admitted it.

As we'd rinsed the sand off of our bodies, I could clearly see that Owen wasn't...disinterested. At least his cock wasn't. He'd been hard and long and it had taken some willpower not to reach across to stroke the outline through his bathing suit.

I'm not a horn dog. It's just that it had been a long time – too long, frankly – since I had been that aroused by a man. I'd been considering having sex on a beach, for heaven's sake. That's how turned on I was. Luckily for both of us, Owen had had the presence of mind to call a halt because if we'd gone through with it…

Complications and questions.

Had he been carrying condoms? I wasn't.

If we had sex, what did it mean? If anything.

I'd been okay so far with the whole idea of a casual relationship with Owen. A sort of vacation romance. Enjoy and savor it, and then when the time came, say goodbye with no regrets or sadness. What did Owen have in mind? I didn't have a clue.

But I was standing in front of Owen's hotel room door only a few feet from my own. My gaze kept shooting back and forth between the two and my brain was calculating how quickly I could make a run for it and hide. That's right, folks, because I'm a lily-livered little shit. For all my bluster and talk about control and practicality, what I am is a coward. This was why I avoided romance quite a bit unless the male was truly compelling.

Like Owen. I'd never met anyone like him. Intense and laidback all at the same time. Intelligent and sexy, too.

Here goes nothing…

Raising my hand to knock, I paused for a moment and took a deep breath before rapping firmly on the door. One. Two. Three times.

I heard footsteps on the other side of the door and then it swung open to reveal Owen in a different pair of casual cargo shorts – olive green – and a black t-shirt with white writing over the pocket.

Symphonic. His dating app.

It was a jolting reminder that this man had millions of women at his fingertips. What was he doing with me? If he believed in his test so deeply, wouldn't that be how he'd want to meet the woman of his dreams?

Stop driving yourself crazy. This is how people end up in rubber rooms drawing pictures with non-toxic crayons.

"Emmy, come in." Owen, his hair slightly damp from a shower, stepped back so I could enter. He smelled clean and delicious. "You're right on time. The pizza should be here any minute."

The hotel had pizza delivery and I'd heard it was pretty decent. When Owen had suggested we try it along with a movie I'd quickly said yes. Then I wondered whether I should have said no, or even just played hard to get.

No, I hated games and wasn't the type. If I wanted to have sex with a man, then I did it.

What I didn't understand was why I was having so many issues with *this* man. Practically from the first moment I'd laid eyes on him I'd been thinking about what it would be like to make love with him, but for some reason I was reticent to simply go for it. While putting on my makeup tonight, I'd given myself quite the talking to.

If you want to have sex with him, then just do it. Why are you acting so strangely?

"I'm starved," I replied, realizing he'd been waiting for me to say something. The silence had stretched on until it was awkward. "I went to the gym when we came back from the picnic."

Then took a shower and promptly fell asleep for a two-hour

nap.

"Ambitious. I'm afraid I just worked a little. I had a few calls to make."

I settled onto the surprisingly comfortable couch. "Who runs the business when you're not there?"

"I have a terrific team of people that can handle pretty much any emergency. At this point, I've stepped back from the day to day business operations to concentrate on my research and refining our matching process."

"The test?"

He nodded and sat down next to me, his thigh brushing mine. I fussed with the throw pillow to cover up my shiver in response.

"The test is our differentiator. We're not just a dating app. We're truly trying to help a client find the love of their life."

"A soulmate."

His smile widened and he reached out to brush the hair out of my eyes. "We're not going to do this again, are we? I don't want to argue with you tonight."

"I don't want to argue, either. I didn't think we were arguing before," I said. "It was more like a healthy debate."

A knock on the door, far more tentative then mine had been. "There's nothing wrong with that unless it upsets the digestion."

"Think I might win the debate?"

Owen stood and headed for the door. "I didn't realize how competitive you are, Emmy, but I like it. I'm not afraid of losing, if that's what you're asking. If you want to know about our methods, fire away. I have no secrets. From you. Now our competitors are a different story. You're not planning to start a dating website, are you?"

"Not in the least. I'll let you put them together, and then I'll get them married."

"We make a good team."

It was a dangerous thought.

★ ★ ★

Owen

EMMY ASKED GOOD questions. Intelligent, thoughtful, and yes, challenging at times. If I hadn't already been attracted to her, I would be now.

We'd finished dinner while chatting about my work. She appeared to be genuinely interested and honestly, I loved talking about it. She might be sorry she'd brought up the subject.

I placed the food tray outside the hotel room door. "How about a movie?"

When I'd issued the dinner and a movie invitation, I hadn't really been thinking all that clearly. My brain's blood supply had still been pooled in my cock and I'd blurted out the first thing that had come into my mind so that I could continue to spend more time with her. It was only later that I'd realized the implications…

Netflix and chill.

As if I was expecting to get laid tonight.

To be completely accurate? I was hoping to, not expecting. I still wasn't sure if I hadn't ruined it all on the beach today. Emmy had been quiet during the picnic lunch, although she'd brightened back up later.

"That sounds fine."

Picking up the remote, I paged through the offerings. "Action? Comedy? Romance?"

"Choose whatever you'd like to watch."

"You don't want to watch a film?"

"It's fine," she assured me, tucking her legs under her. She'd kicked off her shoes and her bare toes peeked out, painted a bright cherry red. "I'm just not picky. You can choose."

"You're not in the mood to watch television."

I didn't phrase it like a question because it wasn't. I was a psychologist and supposedly I could read people. Honestly, Emmy was an open book. She shouldn't quit her day job to take up professional poker, if you know what I mean.

She opened her mouth to correct me but then sighed. "No, I'm not. Is that okay?"

"It's fine. What do you want to do?"

That question hung heavily in the air between us, flashing on and off like an annoying neon sign.

Shit.

"I could call the front desk and see if they have a deck of cards or a board game," I offered hurriedly. In less than a minute, the tension had shot through the roof, as had the temperature. I was sweating through my t-shirt. "Or we could just talk. I'd like to hear more about your business."

Emmy didn't look at me, seemingly fascinated by the hem of her shirt. Pleating it between her fingers, she dared a glance at me, then her gaze dropped again.

"We could...go to bed."

She'd said the words so softly I almost wasn't sure that I

heard them correctly. It was my vivid imagination that had conjured up that statement. A wishful mind had twisted my hearing.

The problem was that all the blood had immediately rushed down to my cock and my mind was sluggish. Forming words was tantamount to a miracle.

"What?"

Okay, I wasn't eloquent. Hell, my vision had gone blurry and I was sure that I'd had a stroke.

This time she looked up, our gazes colliding. Licking her lips nervously, she said it again.

"We could go to bed. You know…together."

Did she honestly think I was going to say no? Hadn't she noticed that I'd been following her around with my tongue hanging out?

Fuck yes, we could go to bed together. If I had anything to say about it, I wouldn't let her out until our flight Monday morning.

Play it cool. Act like you're not ready to jump up and do an end zone dance. She'd hate that.

"We could do that."

Damn straight. I was the luckiest son of a gun in the Caribbean tonight. I loved it when a woman went after what she wanted. It was sexy as hell.

Emmy Grant was full of wonderful surprises.

CHAPTER TWELVE

Emmy

I'D DONE IT. I'd said what I wanted. Inspired by Shelby's book, I'd opened my mouth and told Owen that I wanted to have sex with him. I hadn't been particularly assertive about it but we were now lying on his bed so it must have worked.

To be honest, with as much tension as there was between us, plus what happened on our picnic, I think he was feeling the same way. He'd simply been too much of a gentleman to say it out loud. As he'd offered me movie choices, I'd realized that we were going to sit there watching a film that neither one of us was particularly interested in all because we were too scared to make the first move.

What had Shelby's book said? It had said that we fool ourselves. We think we're going after what we want, but in reality we're sitting back hoping that somebody else takes all the chances. So, I took a leap of faith and now Owen is standing by the bed stripping off his t-shirt.

Ohhhh.... Nice.

He always looked and smelled good to me but watching him stand there and strip was incredibly erotic. Just the mere sight of his naked chest was sending tingles to all the right places.

Did I mention his chest? Wide shoulders, flat abs, with those indentations near the hip bones that made females stupid. What was it called? Oh right, the Adonis Belt. Aptly named, might I say.

He'd popped open his shorts, the sound of his metal zipper loud in the quiet room, the only sound the whirring of the air conditioner. The garment slid down his muscular legs and pooled at his feet. He kicked them away without a backward glance. All he was wearing now was a pair of navy blue boxers.

Scratch that. All he was wearing was a pair of navy blue boxers with a huge imprint of his quite large cock.

I'd seen my share of male anatomy through the years, starting when I was nine and me and Tommy Gibbs from next door had played "doctor" in my garage. I'd played a version of that game on and off with a few boyfriends in high school before losing my virginity in my senior year to a budding thespian who had played Romeo in the school play. I'd been dating fairly regularly in my adult years as well.

Yet never in my life had I wanted a man more than I did Owen Campbell. Right now, at this very moment. It was a physical ache in my belly that was only going to be eased one way.

I wasn't sure I was going to be able to take it slow and savor the moment, to be honest, because I had the sudden urge to grab the waistband of those boxers and rip them down, exposing all the bounty that lay beneath the cotton fabric.

Take chances. Go after what you want.

"Come closer."

I could hear Owen's indrawn breath at my bold words and

then he practically ripped off his boxers, tossing them over his shoulder. His hard cock bobbed free and I gulped at what had been revealed. Long and thick, it reached almost to his bellybut-ton.

Tugging at his hand, I pulled him down on the mattress with me, our bodies tangling together as our lips met in a carnal kiss that was hotter than lava. It was so good it almost made me forget all the things I wanted to do to him. But not quite.

Pressing his shoulders to the bed, I threw my leg over his thighs so I was straddling him. His hands came up to grasp my hips.

"What are you–"

Leaning down, I dropped a few kisses on his chest. "Relax, I'm just having some fun."

His eyebrow quirked and his smile widened. "Fun? Far be it for me to object to that. Have all the fun you want."

He tucked his hands behind his head and grinned up at me. He was laid out naked as the day he was born. All for me.

My goal was obvious but I decided to take my time getting there. I was supposed to be savoring this and so far, I hadn't done a great job with that. Beginning my journey at his neck, I pressed kisses and nibbles on the strong cords of his neck, over his shoulders, and then down to one of his flat male nipples. Swiping my tongue around the circle, I heard his swift intake of breath and then a strangled moan. I liked it so much that I repeated the action on the other side before kissing a path down his flat abs all the way to his treasure trail.

Another part of a man that was aptly named.

His fingers had tangled in my hair and he definitely was

urging me to move faster. Tossing aside my determination to make him wait, I instead ran my tongue up his cock from base to tip. Then I did it again, loving the groan that was torn from his throat.

"Honey," he said hoarsely, his fingers tightening in my hair. "It's not that I don't love what you're doing because damn, I do, but if you keep doing it this evening is going to come to a much earlier conclusion than I'd originally planned."

"We could just start all over again," I replied playfully, dropping a kiss on the wet tip and then swiping my tongue in a circle, drawing another moan from him. "I'm okay with it."

His chuckle was deep and dark. "I'm fine with it too, and I sure as hell like your enthusiasm. But I still think that we should switch places. There's a whole bunch of things I want to do to you, too."

I couldn't deny that I'd been fantasizing about that as well. In fact, I'd stared at his hands far too much at the beach today. Thank goodness he hadn't noticed because I was sure that would come across as creepy. Really, really strange.

Without another word, he grasped my hips again and quickly flipped me on my back before I could even catch my breath. I let out an *oof* as I hit the mattress but I didn't get the chance to complain. Owen was popping open the button on my shorts and sliding them down my legs, leaving a wet path of kisses all the way to my toes. Who knew ankles were so erogenous?

The temperature in the room had zoomed higher in the last ten minutes. Ripping my t-shirt over my head, I tossed it away and went to work on my bra but Owen's fingers brushed mine away.

"Let me," he whispered into my ear before giving the earlobe a nip with his teeth. "I've been fantasizing about doing this since the day I met you."

That day in the bar. I'd had a few dreams myself.

The blood rushed through my veins and roared in my ears as my bra and panties seem to melt away under his tender ministrations. His rough palms cupped my breasts and his thumbs strummed at the hard points, sending arrows of pleasure straight to my clit. A coil of arousal had taken up residence in my lower abdomen and it only tightened further when Owen's lips wrapped around my pebbled nipples. Grabbing the back of his head, I silently urged him on, arching my back and letting my eyelids flutter closed.

He didn't let the other rosy tip go unattended, his tongue dancing around until I was squirming under his muscular frame. So good. Flames licked at my flesh and it was as if I was on fire from the inside out.

Pushing my legs apart, he slid down farther until I could feel his warm breath on my inner thigh. He traced patterns with his tongue on the sensitive skin there, driving me closer and closer to the edge but never letting me go over. He pressed first one, and then a second digit inside my tight channel and rubbed at the sweet spot with his fingertips as his tongue meandered its way through my folds and right to my swollen clit.

It was like being touched by lightning.

White lights flashed behind my lids and I didn't so much as fall over the precipice as jump, my body no longer under my control. Owen was the maestro and he played me easily, keeping me suspended in air until I couldn't take it any longer. At some point, I called out his name in raw need and then he was there, his cock hard against my thigh.

"Honey, just one minute."

He was half off the bed for a moment and then he was back. The sound of crinkling foil told me what his errand had been. I was grateful that at least one of us was thinking clearly.

Then he was nudging at my entrance, pausing as he hovered above me, and capturing my lips with his own.

"Are you sure, Emmy?"

I'd had some terrible taste in men in the past but this one might just break that string of losers. If I'd said no, I knew without a doubt that Owen would stop. He might not be happy about it, but he would.

That wasn't what I was going to say.

"I am, Owen. Yes."

I needed him inside of me more than I needed my next breath. Wrapping my legs around his slim hips, I urged him on. He pressed forward and I could barely breathe. Stretched and full. Incredibly blissful. My nails dug into his shoulders and my legs tightened as he began to pull out and then thrust back in, slowly at first but then picking up speed as we found our rhythm.

Gasps and moans punctuated by the sound of flesh slapping against flesh. It was hot, raunchy, and not at all sweet and romantic. We couldn't seem to get enough of one another and I heard myself begging him to fuck me harder and faster. Anything to make me come again. He obliged, his teeth gritted together and his lips pulled back in a snarl. The pleasure was so acute it was almost painful as it built in my belly. I needed…something…and I would climax spectacularly but it was shimmering just out of my reach.

My fingers anchored onto his ass, trying to direct his strokes. Owen seemed to pick up on my frustration.

“Can you not come, honey? Do you need a little help?”

I didn’t know how to tell him what I needed but thankfully he seemed to get it. Angling his body, he snapped his hips forward so he slid over my clit with each thrust. Perfection. I came apart in his arms a minute later, my soul shattering into a million shiny pieces that looked like stars as they whirled around the room.

Owen followed me over the cliff, his body stiffening and then collapsing on top of me. Our skin was damp with sweat and our limbs in a tangle. Stroking his back, I tried to get my breathing back under control, taking oxygen into my starved lungs. Eventually he rolled off of me and quickly took care of the condom before coming back to bed and cuddling close.

Big spoon and little spoon. He pulled the covers over our rapidly cooling bodies.

“Are you okay? Do you need anything?”

Was I okay? The sex had been…indescribable. Far better than I’d ever imagined. I didn’t have the words to express the myriad of emotions that were running riot inside of me at the moment. Honestly, I didn’t want to talk about my feelings and things I couldn’t quite comprehend.

“I’m fine.”

It wasn’t a lie. I’d wanted this and now we’d done it. I didn’t know what it meant or how I was supposed to feel but I did know one thing to be true.

We'd barely finished and I already wanted to do it again.

I WAS NORMALLY in a pretty decent mood in the morning but today I had a smug grin on my face a mile wide. Emmy had spent the night in my bed and damn, did that woman pack a punch. For someone as uptight as she was most of the time, she knew how to let her hair down when it came to sex. She'd knocked me sideways – twice – last night and I still hadn't recovered.

Stretching and yawning I placed my hand on the bedsheets where she'd lain. Still warm but she was nowhere in sight. Sitting up, I could see her clothes still strewn where we'd tossed them last night. She wasn't in the living room area so that left only one location. I walked over to the bathroom door and heard the sound of water. She was taking a shower.

I knocked quietly but there was no answer. Slowly turning the doorknob, I peeked inside, not wanting to scare the hell out of her but also kind of wanting to surprise her in the shower. The thought of water running down her gorgeous naked body was almost more than I could bear. My cock was hard and ready for action. How did Emmy feel about morning sex?

Me? I'm not that fussy about the time of day, and she could persuade me at any hour.

Pushing the door open wider, steam billowed out of the room revealing my fantasy – a naked Emmy behind a glass shower door. Of course, I couldn't see her clearly through it, but

I was practically salivating at the thought of pressing her up against the marble tiles and fucking us both into paradise.

"Shut the door. You're letting the warm air out."

So much for surprising her.

"I was wondering how late you'd sleep," she said, opening the shower door a crack but I couldn't see her face. "Are you going to join me?"

Fuck yes, I was going to join her. Did she actually think I might turn her down?

I hadn't put any clothes back on after we'd made love the second time so I didn't have any to shed. There was more than enough room for both us and maybe a couple more, if we'd been so inclined. There were two shower heads, one on the wall and one handheld that hooked next to the tiled bench on the far side. I has a few ideas as to how to put the latter to good use.

"Are you still half asleep?"

Shaking my head, I turned my attention to the woman in front of me instead of scouting out locations to fuck. Sometimes the male mind was truly a one-way highway. Her light brown hair was lathered up with shampoo and some of the bubbles ran down her body, creating a sexy peek-a-book effect that left me almost speechless. And painfully hard.

"I wake up slowly. I need a shower and some black coffee before I'm completely human."

Emmy tipped her head back and rinsed the shampoo from her hair. I watched fascinated at an act that she probably did every single day but to me looked more erotic than if she had pole danced onstage covered in glitter.

"I love mornings," she said, reaching for a bottle of conditioner but I managed to beat her to it. I wanted to run my fingers through her wet silky hair. "What are you doing?"

"Helping."

Squeezing a dollop into my palm, I rubbed my hands together and then ran them down the long strands.

"Do you do this a lot?" she asked with a laugh, tipping her head back to rinse it again. "You're pretty good."

"It's nice to know if this psychology thing doesn't work out that I have options."

"You could be a hairdresser, an exotic dancer, or based on the picnic yesterday you could even try your hand at event planning."

Emmy was a little goofy before she'd had her coffee. It was cute.

"An exotic dancer? How did you come up with that profession? Was it all the sequins in my wardrobe?"

Her fingers brushed my abdomen. "I think you'd make a great exotic dancer."

If my cock hadn't already been rock hard it would definitely be now. She was giving me *the look*, that one that told me she was in the mood. Funny how we hadn't known one another all that long but I could pick that expression out easily.

"I'm not the greatest dancer."

Those daring fingers strayed lower, wrapping around my cock. Holy fuck, this woman was bold. "I think you have excellent…rhythm."

"So do you."

My words came out strangled but it was because she'd moved lower, cupping my balls in her dainty hands. Shit, I was already ready to blow and she'd barely touched me. I was like a teenager with my first girlfriend. Emmy was going to think that I had no self control at all.

"Honey, you're playing with fire."

She looked up at me, a smile playing on her full lips. "Really? I thought I was playing with your–"

"Emmy," I interrupted. Cupping her full breasts in my palms, I bent down to nibble at her neck. "You have a dirty mouth. Did you know that?"

She nodded solemnly but I could tell she wanted to laugh. "I do. Are you complaining? Should I be more ladylike?"

One of my hands strayed lower over her belly and between her legs. Jesus, she was wet and ready for me. "Fuck no. I like you just the way you are. In fact, I think you're perfect."

My fingers found her clit, running circles around it. Emmy responded instantly, a moan escaping from her parted lips.

"I'm so close," she whispered and I was barely able to hear her over the sound of the shower. "Fuck me."

I wanted to do just that but…

"I don't have anything. We used the only two condoms I brought with me."

I wasn't expecting to meet anyone on the island and start a torrid affair. I needed to make a trip down to the gift shop.

"Dammit," she muttered under her breath. "We'll have to be more creative, that's all."

More creative turned out to be code words for the blow job to end all blow jobs. Emmy sunk to her knees and proceeded to drive me out of my mind. Her hot mouth, her flitting tongue, the warm water beating down on my back and shoulders while her fingers kneaded my balls. It took an embarrassingly short amount of time and I was groaning her name and holding onto the wall for dear life. I had to lock my knees to stay upright as I climaxed hard, my teeth gritted together. When it was done, I had to sit down on the bench to collect myself.

Emmy redirected the spray so that we wouldn't get cold and then sat down next to me.

"Are you okay?"

"I'm so okay that in about ten seconds I'm going to return the favor. You'll be screaming my name before we're done."

Her eyes lit up with mischief. "Ten…nine…eight…seven…six…"

This amazing woman was counting the time down. I could so fall in love with her.

"One," I said loudly before swiftly moving to my knees. I spread her thighs and draped them over my shoulders. "Just in case you've forgotten, my name is Owen. Everyone in this goddamn hotel is going to know it."

At first, we were both laughing but things quickly turned serious as I pressed two fingers inside of her, moving them in and out while my tongue lapped at her clit. As she'd predicted she was incredibly close. I could feel her walls tightening and hear her breath coming in pants. With a few brushes over her swollen pearl she fell over the cliff, my name echoing off the tile walls. The other guests might not hear it but it was music to my ears.

One look at her post-orgasm and my heart squeezed in my chest. She was totally blissed out, her eyes heavy lidded and her lips curled into a smile. She was so fucking beautiful it made my stomach hurt.

I was falling. Hard. Emmy Grant just might be the one.

CHAPTER THIRTEEN

Emmy

I HAD THE appetite of a lumberjack. So far, I'd put away three pancakes, two strips of bacon, one piece of toast, and a partridge in a pear tree.

Okay, I didn't eat a bird but my plate was beginning to look sparse. Sex was a good workout and amazingly fantastic sex was a great workout. I couldn't begin to imagine how many calories I'd burned last night and this morning. Maybe Shelby needed to add a chapter to her book about sex as a couple's workout.

Owen had also some damage to his meal. He'd ordered the traditional bacon, eggs, and toast along with a yogurt parfait with fruit and granola. He'd quickly drank his orange juice practically in one gulp – dehydration, I assume – and was now emptying his second cup of coffee.

He must have thought I wasn't paying attention because he reached for my last slice of bacon and got a rap on the knuckles with my fork in return.

"I really like you, Owen, but I don't share my food."

Laughing, he settled for his own toast. "You'll share your body with me but not your bacon."

"That's right," I agreed readily. "Because it's bacon. You

don't mess with another person's bacon."

"So if I had tried to steal a piece of pancake or toast that would have been okay?"

I shook my head. "No, I wouldn't have shared that, either."

"Because…?" he prompted, spreading grape jelly on his last slice of toast.

"Because I'm hungry."

"Are you always this possessive about your food?"

"Always."

"Good to know. Just for your information, if you'd asked nicely, I would have given you some of my bacon. We can always order more. I doubt the kitchen has run out."

I was tempted but then I remembered that I didn't want to have to be rolled out of the restaurant.

"I'm full, but I wouldn't mind more coffee."

Like the expensive resort that it was, a waitress holding a coffee carafe seemed to appear out of thin air.

"Would you like more coffee?"

"Yes, please," I replied as she filled up my cup with the dark, steamy goodness. "Thank you so much."

The waitress leaned down and gave Owen a big smile. And a view of her low-cut blouse.

"How about you? More coffee?"

"Actually, I'm good." He glanced over his shoulder toward the kitchen. "I'd really like a glass of water. I don't suppose you could find our waitress?"

"No need. I can get that for you. Or anything else you might want."

Crap, it was barely nine in the morning and Owen was getting hit on by a horny waitress. What in the ever-loving hell? Apparently, I was invisible.

"Just water, thank you. I appreciate it."

The server sashayed back to the kitchen and to Owen's credit he didn't watch her.

"Maybe she thought I was your sister."

Frowning, Owen raised an eyebrow. "I'm not following. Who thinks you're my sister?"

"The waitress." I nodded toward the kitchen. "She offered you *anything else you might want.* I'm guessing she was on the menu if that's what your appetite was in the mood for."

"Emerson Grant, are you jealous? Because I barely noticed that girl. She's far too young for me."

He'd paid enough attention to know that she was young.

"I am not jealous," I replied with a heavy sigh. "I simply think that certain behavior is sort of fascinating. That girl poured coffee for me so she knew I was sitting here across from you. For all she knew, we were married. But that didn't stop her from hitting on you. As a psychologist you don't find that interesting? Because I do."

"Okay, you've piqued my interest." Owen sat back in his chair, tapping his chin in thought. "Let's go through the possibilities. Maybe you read the situation wrong. Or perhaps she likes causing trouble between husband and wife. There's also the possibility that you mentioned. That she thought we were siblings instead of a couple. But I think the most likely explanation is that she gets bigger tips when she flirts with a male."

"That does make sense," I admitted. "But if I were the jealous type, or even worse, if you were the kind of guy to take her up on her offer this could turn out badly for the young woman."

"Agreed. She might only flirt with men she knows are harmless."

"How can she possibly know? She's never spoken two words to you before that exchange."

"People can have a sixth sense about it," Owen shrugged. "When you meet people, do you get a gut feeling about them?"

"I do but sometimes I'm wrong. Here she comes with your water. Let's see if she does it again."

Without so much as a glance toward me, the young woman placed the glass down in front of Owen, once again bending low so her assets were on display.

"Is there anything else I can get you?"

"I'm fine here," he replied before reaching for my hand across the table. "How about you, honey? Is there anything you need?"

"I'm fine."

I barely had the second word out before the server was gone, filling coffee cups all over the dining room.

"So what's the diagnosis, Doctor? Does she flirt with everyone or just the sexy men?"

"It's hard to tell. I still maintain it's for tips."

"You're probably right."

"I didn't encourage her."

I took a sip of my coffee. "I know and I appreciate that. Not all of the men I've gone out with have done the same."

"Assholes," he muttered under his breath. "I hope you dumped every one of them right away."

"I did. I probably could have saved myself some time if I had a nifty test like you do. Put the guys through their paces before I agreed to a date."

"A nifty test? Is that what you think I do for a living?" Luckily, he wasn't offended at all. In fact, he found the description amusing because he was laughing. "It's a little more scientific than that."

"I'd have my own test and I wouldn't need a PhD to put it together, either."

Leaning forward, he rested his elbows on the table. "Do go on. I'm intrigued."

"First, I'd take him to one of those restaurants where all the waitresses wear tight cut off t-shirts and short-shorts."

"And then?"

"Then I'd have him meet my friends and their pets. If they don't like him, then that's it. I'd also observe him in his own natural habitat, of course."

Owen almost choked on his ice water. "His habitat?"

"Absolutely. See what his home looks like. Is he a slob? Does he throw his laundry on the floor? Doe he only eat pizza and Chinese takeout while he plays video games? Those are deal breakers. Also, I'd want to see him hang out with his friends. How does he act? Does he revert to being a teenager? And I'd want to see him interact with his own family as well. How he treats his mother is a huge indicator as to how he'll treat me. Believe me when I say that I've seen some grooms treat their own mothers like dirt. It's shameful."

"You've given this topic a great deal of thought."

Fiddling with my coffee cup, I nodded in agreement. "I have, actually. I see couples each and every day of my life and I guess I'm a little jaded. I've seen some things that would curl your hair."

"But there are happy couples?" he pressed. "Couples that restore your faith?"

"Sure, like Lisa and Dan, but not everyone is as wonderful as they are. In your line of work, you have to see it too, right?"

"I do, but I guess that I concentrate on the ones that work and not the ones that don't."

"So I told you about my test. Tell me about yours," I challenged, waggling my eyebrows. "What sort of questions do you ask? What do you need to know to put two people together?"

Owen's smile widened. "If you're really interested, I can make arrangements for you to take the test. What do you say?"

Yes, I was that curious. Call me crazy but I wanted to know.

"I say yes. Let's do it." I raised my hand when he was going to speak again. "I assume that you have also taken this test?"

He nodded.

"Then what happens if we're not compatible?"

"Honey, I guarantee you that we're compatible."

I wasn't sure that I even believed in this so-called scientific test.

"But what if we're not?"

"We will be," he promised. "Don't you trust me?"

I wanted to, but my cynicism ran deep.

"When can I take the test?"

"As soon as I pay the check."

No time like the present. Too bad I didn't study for this.

Emmy

We were back in Owen's suite and he'd set up his laptop on the small desk near the window. All the way back to the room, I'd become increasingly nervous. There was no passing or failing but since he owned the company, he would have access to my answers which I assumed would be to rather personal questions. It was more frightening than being naked in front of him. This was far more revealing.

"Is there a time limit?" I asked when I sat down at the desk. The website was open to the welcome screen. "What if I want to change my answer?"

"There's no time limit and you can change any answer before submitting. The test takes most people about thirty minutes but you can take as long as you like. Some people take it but don't submit it right away. They come back to it later in the day or the next and make any changes then."

Half an hour wasn't bad. It was longer than a pop quiz but less than a test in high school, which usually took a full hour.

I reached for the mouse and then glanced over my shoulder where Owen was still hovering. "Are you going to stand there and watch me? Because that's a little creepy, to be honest."

"Yes. Right. How about I step out onto the balcony and make a few calls?"

"That's fine. I'll let you know when I'm done."

He took a few steps and then hesitated at the sliding glass doors. "Don't overthink the questions. Usually your first instinct is the best answer."

"Okay."

He still didn't move.

"Don't think about how you'd like things to be. Think about how they actually are."

Geez Louise.

"Got it."

"If you need–"

"Owen," I interrupted, giving him a sweet smile. "I can't start the test until you step outside."

Color washed across his cheeks. "Sorry. I just get a little nervous about this. It's sort of my baby, after all."

"I'll treat it with love and care."

Then a thought occurred to me.

"Wait…are you worried that we won't be compatible?"

"I am not."

He didn't look sure.

"Because it wouldn't matter to me. I'm the one that's skeptical, remember? You're the one that believes in this."

Sighing, he crossed his arms over his chest. "It's not voodoo, Emmy. It's science. The good thing about science is that it's true whether you believe in it or not."

"You make a valid point. Now…shoo."

Owen finally stepped out onto the patio and I started work.

1. *What one word describes you best?*

Busy.

Emmy

I THOUGHT SHELBY was going to have a cow, right there on Skype.

"You took the test? What was it like? Do you have the results yet?"

"I did take the test this morning," I confirmed, relaxing in my room later that day. Owen had a business conference call so I'd decided to call Shelby and see what was going on back home. "It wasn't too bad."

The test wasn't the ordeal that I'd feared it would be. In fact, many of the questions didn't appear to have anything to do with relationships at all. Knowing Owen, those were probably the most important.

"That doesn't tell me anything."

"What do you want to know?"

"Tell me about the questions," Shelby demanded, her tone huffy. "You know that's what I'm interested in. I think this is fascinating."

"You could take the test yourself," I pointed out. "You don't have to do anything with the results. I'm sure Brad would understand that you did it for science."

"Brad would understand. Now tell me about the test."

Briefly I told her as much as detail as I could remember and received the requisite ooh and ahhs in return. She was acting like Owen was in a famous boy band.

"When do you get your results? What if you're not compatible with Owen Campbell?" Now she sounded panicky. "That would be awful. Maybe you shouldn't have taken the test."

"Since this version of the test is a beta they've been working on, the 'scoring' doesn't happen immediately. I will get my results in a few days. As for us being a match, Owen explained to me that our being compatible wasn't a yes or no answer. The system scores matches on a continuum. We might be eighty percent compatible or only fifty percent. But he's absolutely positive that we'll be some sort of match."

"Wouldn't it be great if you were a one hundred percent match?"

"No such thing. I asked."

"That's disappointing. I would love to talk to some of those couples."

"I can't even imagine what a match like that would be like. Would they dress and talk the same? Finish each other's sentences?"

"Perhaps they could read each other's minds," Shelby suggested with a laugh. "Although that might be dangerous. I wouldn't want my significant other to be able to read my mind."

Me neither.

"How is your bride feeling, by the way?" Shelby asked. "Is she any better?"

"Lisa? She's feeling pretty awful but Dan is taking care of her. They think she might be on the upswing, however, and she might get to taste some of her wedding cake tomorrow if she continues to improve. So what's going on back home? Did we get more snow?"

"Emerson Marie Grant, are you kidding me? You're asking about the weather? It's cold. How does that sound? Now get to what's really important. Your date last night. It must have gone well if you took the test this morning. Tell me every detail and don't leave anything out."

"You're not getting every detail."

Shelby's eyes went round onscreen and her smile widened. "That good, huh? Start at the beginning. What happened?"

My friend wasn't going to let this go.

"I went to his suite for dinner and then we were going to watch a movie. But…"

"But," she prompted. "He didn't want to watch a movie?"

There wasn't much my friends didn't know about my life and vice versa. What the hell.

"I didn't want to watch a movie and I really got the feeling that he didn't either so…"

If possible, her eyes grew even bigger.

"So you…found other activities?" she suggested delicately. "Horizontal ones?"

"We were horizontal last night. This morning we were definitely vertical."

I should have known by now that Shelby was unshockable. She'd heard too many wild things in her private practice to ever blink an eye at whatever we got up to.

"Good for you," she replied, clapping her hands together in delight. "How was it?"

"They haven't invented words to describe it yet."

All the adjectives that I could have used would have been too weak.

"You lucky duck. So you had amazing sex last night and this morning. Then you took the matching test. Will there be wedding bells in the near future?"

Whoa. Just…hold the phone.

"Wedding bells?" I echoed, rolling my eyes. "We just met a few days ago. I would hardly think that we'd be talking about getting married."

"He isn't the kind of man that you could have a future with?"

"That's not the point." This was awkward. "From what I know about him so far, he's definitely the kind of guy that I could get serious about. *Sometime in the future.* It's too soon to be talking about love."

Shelby's mouth twisted. "Because you don't believe in love at first sight. Or even second, third, fourth, or fifth sight."

We'd been through this a million times but it looked like we were going to do it again.

"Love at first sight is just lust and infatuation," I explained patiently. "You can't possibly love someone that you don't know."

"And yet, we hear stories about it all the time."

"No, we hear stories about couples who fall in lust at first sight and manage to fall in love later. Don't get the two confused. If Owen and I continue this relationship when we return to Arborville–"

"If? Is there any question about that?"

"If we decide to continue," I kept going as if she hadn't said anything. "Then we will spend time with one another, learn about one another, and at some appropriate time in the future make the decision to take the relationship to the next level or end things in a civilized manner."

Groaning, Shelby slapped her forehead. "And what, pray tell, is the next level?"

"You know…being in love. Meet the family. Talk about the future."

"But you're not going to think about the future until you both decide to take it to the next level? How very rational and practical of you."

"I'm a very rational and practical person," I replied icily. "Come on, as a psychologist you have to see couples every day that didn't think it through and now they have two kids, a dog, a mortgage, and a minivan while the entire time they tell you that they really don't love each other anymore. I'm just making sure that I'm not one of them."

"I do see them," Shelby readily agreed. "But at least they could say they'd been in love. They've experienced the highs and lows that life and love have to offer. Not every great love has a happy ending."

"That's the most depressing statement I've ever heard. If it doesn't end happily, can you really call it a great love? I don't think so."

"Romeo and Juliet."

Uh-uh. No way.

"Two teenagers with a crush that killed six people, including themselves? That's not love, my friend. Try again."

"I don't have anything off the top of my head. Give me some time."

"Fine, take all the time you need."

Shelby leaned toward the camera on her laptop. "You like him, right? Because you look really happy. Glowing, even."

"I am happy," I confirmed. "But that doesn't mean I'm in love."

I would know if I'd fallen in love. Right?

"Do you think about him all the time?"

Well...yes.

"We're in the same hotel on a small island, Shelby. It would be hard not to."

"You are such a hard case, Emmy. You need to let it happen. Enjoy it. Savor the journey. Take a chance."

I'd taken a chance last night and it had worked out pretty well but that didn't mean I needed to be jumping off cliffs all the time. It could easily have gone the other way.

"I know," I replied with a sigh. "I read that in your book and that's what I'm trying to do. I'm enjoying myself. But that doesn't mean that I'm falling in love."

"I think you're fighting it," Shelby said, authority in her tone. It was the one she used when she was in doctor mode. "You need to open yourself to it. That's in the book, too. Did you get that far?"

"No, but I intend to. I got to the part about going after what you want and I did that last night. I also read the part about how to enjoy dating someone without evaluating them as a potential spouse. That's what I'm doing. Having a good time."

"And that's what I want you to do. Just don't deny your feelings."

"I won't," I promised. "But you have to be okay if this relationship doesn't turn into the romance of the century."

"As long as you're okay if it does," Shelby shot back, a gleam in her eye that I could easily see even over a laptop camera.

"Don't fight the magic of love, Emmy. It's so worth it."

The magic of love. Were Shelby and Owen ganging up on me?

I might follow the advice in my friend's book…but I'd fall in love on my own terms.

CHAPTER FOURTEEN

Owen

I WANTED TO make our last evening on the island together as special as possible. I'd spent the last two nights with Emmy in my bed and as far as I was concerned, she could stay there for a hell of a lot longer.

She had all the qualities that I'd hoped for in a woman. Okay, that's going a little too far. Emmy had *most* of the qualities that I was looking for. She definitely had all of the important ones that I couldn't bend on. Smart, funny, kind-hearted, ambitious, and curious. I think it was her curiosity that I adored most of all. The fact that she'd been willing to take *Symphonic's* matching test showed that she was open-minded and wanted to learn about all sorts of things. Despite appearing to the contrary, she wasn't set on one way of thinking.

The fact that she was beautiful and the sex was out of this world didn't hurt either, although I would have been fine if she'd been a hag and the lovemaking so-so. It would have been a disappointment but we certainly could have worked on it together. As for her looks…external beauty fades. But hate and nastiness were bone deep.

I was ready to admit it. I was falling in love. That's why I wanted to make this last evening as romantic and memorable as possible. Luckily, I'd establish a rapport with the concierge who had been filled with ideas. Emmy didn't think she was the traditionally romantic type but after seeing her set up Lisa and Dan's wedding, I thought she was selling herself short.

That's why I was standing in the middle of the hotel lobby, heart in my throat, sweat pooling on the back of my neck. Nervous as hell. I could only hope Emmy would see the effort that had gone into my plans for the evening and it would let her know how I felt about her. I'd never gone to such lengths to impress a female.

"Owen?"

Whirling around, I was riveted in place. Emmy looked gorgeous in a white halter dress that just skimmed the tops of her knees. She'd put her hair up tonight and it showed off her graceful neck and kissable shoulders.

"You look amazing."

I wasn't the most eloquent of men. Emmy's cheeks turned a pretty shade of pink and she clutched her small handbag a little closer to her chest.

"Thank you," she replied huskily. "You look good, too."

I was wearing my best suit, the same that I'd worn to Lisa and Dan's cocktail party a few days ago. I'd told Emmy that we were doing something special and I wanted to look the part.

"Are you ready to go?"

"Go?" she echoed, her gaze darting around the lobby. "Are we leaving the resort?"

"We are," I confirmed. "I hope that's okay."

If it wasn't then we had issues because there was no plan B.

"It's fine," she said quickly. "I just didn't realize, that's all. Where are we going?"

"It's sort of a surprise."

"Oh."

She'd been excited about the surprise last time. This time? Not so much.

"You're not in the mood for a surprise."

Sighing, she wrinkled her nose and shook her head. "I'm really sorry. I have my moments and this is one of them. My friends say I'm difficult. They're probably right."

"You're not too bad," I laughed, linking my arm with hers and leading her down the path toward the marina. Her perfume mixed with the smell of hibiscus. "But since you don't want a surprise tonight, I'll tell you where we're going. I've hired a yacht to take us out on the water around the islands while we eat a gourmet meal under the stars. How does that sound?"

Emmy stopped and stared up at me. "It sounds amazing. Are you kidding?"

"Yes, Emmy. I'm totally joking. We're not going on a yacht. We're going to pick up some fast food and then hit the arcade for the rest of the evening."

"I'll have you know that I am the Ms. PacMan champ among my girlfriends. I play a mean game of air hockey, too."

"If I can find an air hockey table on this island consider yourself challenged to a winner take all match. In the meantime, we're going to have to make do with moonlight and romance."

It was romantic. The for-hire yacht had pulled out all the stops as I'd requested. A rose petal strewn path to the candlelight table on the back of the boat. Soft music in the background.

Champagne on ice. I popped the cork on the bottle as the yacht smoothly glided away from the marina, headed for open water.

Handing her the flute filled with bubbly golden liquid, I lifted my own glass in a toast.

"To us."

Did I mention that I wasn't an eloquent fucker? I didn't have those smooth-talking skills. If that's what Emmy wanted then she was barking up the wrong tree with me.

"To us," she echoed, our glasses clinking together. The chilled liquid slid easily down my throat and the bubbles tickled Emmy's nose, making her giggle. "This is really good."

"You must really know your wines and champagne in your business. You probably have it all the time."

It wasn't that special after all.

"I don't," she said, placing her glass on the dinner table and running her hands up my arms to my shoulders. "I never drink on the job and I don't know that much about wine and spirits. I let others guide me. This is wonderful, Owen."

"Not too over the top romantic?"

Inwardly wincing at my question, I waited for her verdict. She didn't answer right away, her expression conflicted.

"It's lovely, really, really lovely, and I am completely surprised."

"But?"

"But nothing. This is wonderful. Thank you for going to such lengths for us to have a special evening together."

I still wasn't convinced. Blame it on my inner paranoia. But I was going to shut the hell up and not ruin our last night together.

"I'm glad you like it. The food is supposed to be out of this world." Leaning down, I dropped a kiss on her full lips. "I know you like to eat."

"I do." She turned to look out onto the shimmering water. "Do we have a specific destination?"

Inwardly I chuckled. Emmy was so practical and goal-oriented. She'd want to know where we were going and how long it would take to get there. If her GPS gave her an estimated time of arrival, she would want to beat it like an Olympic swimmer.

"No destination. Just cruise around the islands. Isn't it beautiful to look at the lights and the stars?"

"It is beautiful," she agreed, her gaze still trained on the night sky. It was a clear night with a simple warm breeze. "I've been to the Caribbean a few times before but I never get used to how gorgeous it is."

I could say the same about her. She knocked me sideways and made me happy to stay that way. Did she feel the same?

★ ★ ★

Emmy

OWEN'S EVENING RIVALED anything that I could have put together, and I was a professional. He'd pulled out all the stops – rose petals, champagne, good food, soft music. Heck, even the stars and moon had cooperated. He must have them on retainer.

It was all so…romantic. Over the top. Almost cringingly so. Displays such as this always made me slightly uncomfortable. How could I ever live up to it? Did I even want to try?

For his part, Owen seemed happy enough. We'd eaten the delicious food prepared by the onboard chef. Delicate lobster tail dipped in clarified butter. Grilled vegetables with some sort of spicy sauce. A decadent chocolate mousse at the end that I couldn't stop eating no matter how full my stomach.

I'd drank a few more glasses of champagne and was feeling delightfully fuzzy. Not drunk. Just…happy. There were no cares to be had at the moment and tomorrow's departure from the island seemed a long way away.

I was savoring.

I wanted to simply sit back and enjoy this moment with a man that made me tingle. He lifted the champagne bottle and held it over my glass.

"More champagne?"

Shaking my head, I placed my hand over the top of the flute. "I'd better not. I'm already tipsy."

"You're adorable when you're tipsy."

"I'm not sure all of my friends agree with you, Owen. That does not seem to be the prevailing opinion back home."

"They're wrong," he drawled, instead lifting the carafe of ice water and freshening up my glass. "You're sweet and funny. Giggly, too. It's very cute."

It should go without saying that I wasn't normally a giggly female. That wouldn't really match my persona as someone that a client could trust with their event planning needs.

"Ashlyn would never describe me as cute. She's cute, though. She's a petite blonde. Very dainty."

"I haven't heard so much about your other friend Mia. What's she like?"

"Lucky."

The word popped out of my mouth before I could stop it. Not that it wasn't the truth.

"Lucky? How so?"

How to explain this without it sounding crazy? Well...I'll give it a shot.

"Mia was in love with the boy next door, so to speak. This guy Josh, however, had her firmly in the friend zone. It was really heartbreaking for her because he was dating all these women and he was treating her like a pal."

"That is terrible," Owen said with a shake of his head. "What happened? You said she was lucky but that doesn't sound like it."

"I'm getting to that," I said, taking a sip of my water. "She stopped at a convenience store near her house one night and got caught in a robbery. She survived but when she had a gun pointed at her chest, she made a deal with the universe. She was going to go after what she wanted. No more sitting back and waiting. So she went for Josh."

"And?" Owen prompted with a grin. "I have to know the ending. Did she get him or did she find someone even better?"

"She got him," I confirmed. "But she had to be tough on him at first. He was a real ass in the beginning, sort of wishy washy. He wasn't sure he wanted to be in a relationship with her so she packed him off and sent him home. It was so brave of her but she did it. Josh realized what he had and they ended up together. In fact, they're in Scotland right now while she's in a teacher exchange program."

"That's a terrific story. Love always finds a way."

"Spoken like a true romantic," I teased. "For a man who uses a test to put people together, you're awfully fanciful."

His brows shot up and he reached into the pocket of his suit jacket. "Speaking of tests…I have your results, Emmy. Do you want to see?"

I did, and I didn't. From the smile on Owen's face, however, it appeared that we were compatible. That was good. Right?

"Of course, I want to see," I replied, holding out a hand as he pulled out a single sheet of paper. "I've been wondering about it."

Not in the last hour or so but it had been in the back of my mind as the day had gone on. When he didn't say anything by lunch, I'd assumed that the results weren't good and he was going to pretend that I'd never taken the test.

There was just enough light to see the printing on the paper. Scanning it from top to bottom, it was a summary of where Owen and I fell on their continuum.

Sixty-nine percent.

"I have a much more detailed report of your results on my laptop and I'll happily send that to you if you like. Those results are short and to the point."

"Sixty-nine percent. Is that good?"

From his smile it must be but the results didn't really make that clear.

"I think it's very good. Dan and Lisa were at seventy-two percent, only three percentage points higher. Anything over eighty is as rare as hen's teeth, and anything below forty is probably a relationship that may be more work than a person is willing to put in. We don't tell a participant what a good percentage is, though. It's up to them to decide what's acceptable to them."

"But you think it's good?"

"I do."

"Emmy…"

I raised my gaze to see Owen watching me closely.

"Emmy, are you okay?"

"I am."

It was just…what did this mean? Geez, that was such a girly question and I hated myself for even asking it in my head. Where is this relationship going? Does he like me? Do we have a future? Why did this one man make me insecure?

Reaching across the table, he plucked the paper from my hand before taking both of them in his. "Dance with me."

What? Talk about a non-sequitur.

"You want to dance?"

"I do. Will you dance with me, Emmy? Even though I have two left feet?"

There was music playing from invisible speakers. Something slow and sexy that I couldn't identify.

"I will."

He stood and helped me to my feet. There was a small area right next to our table and that's where he pulled me into his arms, pressing my body against his. After two nights in his bed, you'd think being this close to him would be no big deal. Old hat.

It wasn't, though. His scent was still intoxicating, all citrus and spice, turning my knees to jelly. The warmth from his skin permeated the thin material of my dress and it was like being skin to skin. I placed my hands around his neck, my fingertips brushing the tiny curls at his nape. His lips pressed against my temple and the oxygen seemed to leak from my lungs even as my heart kicked into gear. Surely no one could live very long not breathing while their heart beat like a big brass drum in a marching band. It sounded like a lethal combination.

"Emmy…" His voice was soft and low, his lips next to my ear. "I haven't felt this strongly for a woman in a long time. If ever. I don't want this weekend to be the end. I want to keep seeing you when we get home. I want to find out where this goes. I know we haven't discussed what happens after tomorrow but I want to keep seeing you when we go back home. Do you?"

The answer slipped off of my tongue so easily, no effort whatsoever. It was a foregone conclusion.

"Yes, I want that."

CHAPTER FIFTEEN

Emmy

I DON'T REMEMBER much of the rest of the evening. There was champagne, dancing under the stars, and kisses in the moonlight. Nothing too crazy, though. We weren't alone on that yacht and neither one of us was the type to make a spectacle of ourselves.

When we returned to the resort we went straight to my room as if we'd discussed the alternatives and made a decision. We barely spoke in the elevator as it swiftly and silently rose but our steps were rushed as we exited and walked down the hall. The closer we came to the door the faster my heart sped in my chest. I couldn't wait to rip those fancy clothes off of him and push him down on the bed. We only had tonight left.

Scratch that. We were going to continue the relationship back home so theoretically we had many more nights like this. But this one still felt special. There was so much unspoken, hanging in the air between us. We cared about one another to make an effort past tomorrow morning. In my world, that was a big deal. I couldn't remember the last time a man got to me this way.

As soon as the hotel room door swung shut behind us, Owen

flipped the lock on the door and walked me backward straight to the bed, tugging at my clothes on the way. By the time I fell back onto the mattress I wasn't wearing anything but my panties.

His shoulders rose and fell as he stripped off his own clothes and tossed them carelessly aside. He was hard and ready and I hadn't even touched him yet.

I wanted to remedy that slight immediately.

Sitting up on the bed, I reached for him, running a hand up and down his velvety shaft, drawing a tortured moan from his lips. I loved that I could affect him this strongly with the simplest of caresses. It made me feel sexy and powerful and I couldn't wait to do it again. Leaning forward, I swiped around the tip with my tongue as he tangled his fingers in my hair. Taking the head into my mouth, I slowly slid down as far as I could before retreating and lifting back up. I did it twice more before his hands cupped my face and pulled me off with a pop.

"I don't want this to be over yet."

I didn't either but being in control was kind of fun. My fingertips grazed his cock and it jumped, his body shaking with the force of his reaction. Before I could do it again, Owen immediately lifted me and gently tossed me back onto the bed, lowering himself on top and caging me in with his strong arms.

Not that I wanted to escape. I was quite content at the moment to stay exactly where I was.

The moon peeked through a tiny opening in the curtains, throwing a shadow across Owen's face. He was such an amazingly beautiful man. If he'd been born hundreds of years ago, he would have been rendered in marble, his image captured for all to see.

Reaching up, I caressed those high cheekbones and then ran my fingers down the bridge of his nose, slightly crooked as if he'd broken it a long time ago.

"I'd love to tell you that I hurt myself playing football or something macho like that but it would be a lie," he laughed, dropping kisses on my neck and shoulders. Luxuriating in the attention, I let my eyelids flutter shut so I could fully immerse myself in the pleasure. "I fell down a flight of stairs in college helping one of my buddies move. Ended up in the emergency room. It's why I snore."

So far Owen had so thoroughly exhausted me that I'd fallen asleep immediately each night. I'd had no idea that he snored.

"You were doing a friend a favor. That's kind of macho."

His slid an open-mouthed kiss down my torso, between my breasts and over my belly. I could feel his warm breath on my slit and his fingers drawing patterns on the sensitive flesh of my inner thigh. My entire being trembled inside and out while my heart pounded against my ribcage.

"You have a strange definition of macho, honey, but I'll go with it."

If I'd been predicting what Owen was going to do next, I would have been wrong. Turning my expectations on their heads, he scooted to the bottom edge of the bed and lifted up one of my feet. Cradled in his large palm, he leaned down to press a kiss at the sensitive arch, almost sending me up off of the bed in response.

Taking a leisurely path and not in one bit of a hurry, he continued to drop wet kisses on the top of my foot and ankle before following a path up my calves and thighs. Twisting on the mattress, I groaned and sighed with every kiss and caress. His touch was feather light but somehow, he managed to only arouse me and not tickle. Flames licked at my flesh and blood roared in my ears, building my arousal higher until I was panting and dizzy with need.

With an evil smile on his face, he did it all over again with the other leg, his gentle touch moving me closer to the precipice. It wouldn't take much to send me over and I was desperate to fall. My fingers curled into his hair, tugging his head where I wanted it but the bastard wouldn't cooperate. "Don't tease me. It's mean."

He only chuckled and continued his sensual foray, now exploring my rib cage and bellybutton.

"You don't sound like I'm being mean. You sound like you like it. Do you want me to stop?"

No, I didn't unless he was going to do something even better.

Jackpot. His lips finally traveled in the right direction, his shoulders insinuating themselves between my thighs.

With the first touch of his mouth I would have sworn angels sang in the distance. My body bowed on the mattress as his clever tongue did naughty, talented things that had me going up in flames. He lapped at my clit and that was it. I fell over the cliff and didn't look back. White lights strobed behind my lids and the world tilted on its axis. I didn't fight the rush of pleasure, simply letting it take me wherever it wanted me to go. When I finally came down I was limp, panting, and begging. I needed him inside of me now. To my surprise, the orgasm hadn't sated me in the least. I wanted more.

Luckily, Owen seemed to be of the same mind. I heard the crinkle of foil and then he was there right where I needed him. He pushed relentlessly forward, not in a hurry but slowly and deliberately, letting me feel every delicious inch of his invasion. When he was in to the hilt, we both paused for a moment to catch our breath. I was so full of him and it was amazing. I didn't have the words to describe it; I only knew that this wasn't just ordinary sex. This was something different, something better.

"What does it feel like?"

Shit, I couldn't control my mouth at times like this. We didn't need to talk about it, but the thought had drifted through my mind and now I'd actually spoken the words out loud.

"Being inside you?" he asked, his voice hoarse and low, like ground glass. "It feels like heaven. So hot and tight. I never want it to end."

He'd begun to move and that took any thought of answering away. Frankly, it was hard to speak when I could barely breathe. Instead, I wrapped my legs around his lean middle as his strokes sped up, hitting that spot inside of me that made me see stars. He rode me fast and hard and I loved every minute of it, exhorting him along the way. We'd both have bruises in the morning, mine on my hips and his on his shoulders, but they'd be wonderful reminders of our time on the island.

The lewd sounds of fornication rang in our ears – the slapping of damp flesh on flesh, the carnal groans, the ragged breathing. It all added to the pleasure and I found myself once again teetering on the brink, ready to fly into the clouds.

Reaching between us, Owen ran his thumb around my clit. Once, twice, three times. The last time was the charm and I rocketed into space, calling out his name. He followed me right after and I forced myself to keep my eyes open, wanting to see him go over the edge.

His teeth were gritted together, his jaw tight and his head thrown back, exposing the cords of his neck. He was incredibly beautiful and I watched as the pleasure ran through him over and over until we were both wrung out and exhausted.

He collapsed on top of me as we both sucked oxygen into our aching lungs. I ran my fingertips along the damp muscles of his back and simply savored the moment. In my hectic life I didn't often have times like this where I could simply be. I'd spent a good portion of my adult life working and being in charge of every little detail. I wasn't in charge of shit right now and it was fantastic.

Being with Owen might be better than I'd ever thought it could be. We were now in a real relationship, not just a vacation fling.

I'd taken a chance and it had paid off. I was…happy.

CHAPTER SIXTEEN

Emmy

THE PLANE WOULD be landing soon and I would be back to my normal, everyday life.

When I'd woken this morning – cuddled close to Owen in his bed – I'd realized that the fantasy of this little vacation was over and we were returning to reality. Monday morning and time to throw my clothes into a suitcase and board a flight for the snow and cold of the Midwest. The only comfort was that Owen had come with me, at least until Miami. From there we were on different flights. To be on his preferred airline, he had a much longer layover and would be arrive later in the day.

I wasn't the greatest traveler by air. I was constantly frustrated by the hurry-up-and-wait culture in the industry. Add in the uncertainty of weather and mechanical issues and it was a recipe for pulling out my hair one clump at a time. But you can't drive to a Caribbean island so every now and then I had to shut the hell up and deal with it. My friend Ashlyn travels all the time and I don't know how she does it. She's a lot more chill than I am, clearly.

The plane dipped down and hit the runway at Chicago's O'Hare with a few hard bumps that rattled my teeth. My hands clenched the armrests until the plane came to a stop at the airport. I'd arrived alive and in one piece. I could breathe easily again.

Pulling my phone out of a side pocket of my bag, I quickly sent a text to Shelby that my plane had touched down. She was picking me up and driving me the two and a half hours to Arborville. Did I mention that she was an awesome friend? If she hadn't offered, I would have had to leave my own car parked here and the last time I did that I walked around the parking garage for over an hour in the freezing cold dragging a suitcase, a carryon, and a purse before I finally found my vehicle. To this day I swear someone moved it from where I'd left it.

After exiting the plane, I made my way through the hustle and bustle to the baggage claim area. I hadn't checked any bags but Shelby was picking me up here curbside. I'd shot her another text and...

There she was, driving her shiny blue BMW sedan that she'd named Otto. She pulled up and waved, honking her horn in case I wasn't paying any attention. Since she already had four or five cars on her tail, I jumped into her car, shoving my luggage into the backseat.

"Let's go before you get a ticket or rammed from behind by an impatient driver."

Shelby loved to drive Otto – that's why she'd offered to pick me up – and she obediently pressed down on the accelerator, shooting the powerful car forward and into airport traffic. We missed a yellow cab by about three centimeters. I grabbed onto the door handle but Shelby simply laughed.

"I wasn't even close to him. We had plenty of room."

"If you call less than an inch *plenty of room* than yes, you did. Seriously, I'm grateful to you for picking me up but let's get home in one piece, okay? You're going to be a bride soon, so you should have a lot to live for."

My friend only spared me a brief glance as she navigated toward the exit. "Isn't it you that's always reminding me that I only get one day to feel special?"

"I am and that's why you'll want to live to see that one day."

We didn't speak until Shelby was safely on the interstate traveling south. There was nothing between Chicago and Arborville but corn and cows.

"Are you going to talk about it?"

I didn't like to make things too easy for Shelby.

"Talk about what?"

She didn't even take her gaze from the road but I could hear her guffaw of amusement.

"Dr. Owen Campbell, of course. What's the latest? Are you going to see him now that you've both returned home?"

"Oh…that." Settling back into the leather seat, I tried to appear nonchalant. None of this was a big deal, right? "Yes, we're going to continue to date and just see how it goes."

As if the outcome didn't matter to me in the slightest.

"See how it goes? That sounds very…casual. Are you planning to be non-exclusive then?"

Shit, that hadn't occurred to me. I'd assumed… Double shit.

"You two didn't talk about that?" Shelby guessed. "If you'd read the book all the way through you wouldn't have made that mistake."

"Thanks for pointing that out. I've read most of it. I admit that I've skipped around a little."

"So you're not sure if you're an exclusive couple?"

I thought back to everything that Owen had said and done, especially last night. He'd gone all out and it wouldn't make sense to do that for a booty call. Or a hookup. Whatever it was called these days. He'd also said that he hadn't felt this strongly in a long time. That was true for me as well.

"We're exclusive," I finally replied, this time with certainty. "I'm sure of it."

"But you don't know for certain?"

"I don't need to interrogate a man to know, Shel. We're a couple. He made a big deal last night about saying that he wanted to continue our relationship back home and see where it went. I don't need to get it in writing. At some point I need to trust him. At least that's what you'd tell me."

"Agreed, but just make sure that he's as committed to the relationship as you are. That's all I'm saying."

"I will," I promised. "I know you're just trying to make sure I don't get hurt. I'm not sure that I'm really that far gone, if you know what I mean. I'm not in love. Not yet."

Shelby's gaze flickered to me and then back to the road. Reaching down, she turned off the radio that had been humming softly in the background. "You're not in love? You sound quite sure of that."

"I would hope so. I would think that I would know if I was in love, Shel."

I was definitely in lust though, and deep-deep like.

She sighed and shook her head. "Emmy, my friend, you are the last person that would know if you were in love. For all the weddings you've planned, the anniversaries, and the christenings you don't know shit about love, and most especially your own feelings. Love is going to have to hit you over the head and drag you around before you recognize that it has you."

"I didn't realize that you thought I was such a twit," I replied hotly, blowing out a disgusted breath. "Does Mia and Ashley share your low opinion of me or is it just you?"

"I've never discussed it with them. You'll have to ask them for yourself."

I made a mental note to do just that. Shit, I wasn't stupid.

"Dammit, Shel," I said out loud. "I'm not an imbecile."

"You're not," she agreed. "In fact, you're one of the smartest people I know."

That didn't make any sense.

"If I'm so smart then why wouldn't I know that I'm in love? Are you deliberately trying to confuse me?"

"Not at all. What I'm saying is that intelligence isn't the same as romantic intelligence."

"Romantic intelligence," I parroted. "What in the ever-loving fuck is that? Is this something you made up for your book?"

"It's a thing," Shelby replied defensively. "I may have coined the term but that doesn't make it any less real. You can know everything there is to know about the Civil War and still not have the introspection to know when a man is right or wrong for you. Or for example, that you're in love."

I already knew the answer but I asked the question anyway.

"I suppose there's a quiz in your book that would tell me if I'm in love?"

What was it with Owen, Shelby, and their tests?

Frowning, she shook her head. "Um, no. There's a chapter about it, though. That must be one of the ones you skipped over."

"Because I would know if I was in love."

Shelby was passing car after car, her foot firmly on the gas pedal. The scenery was almost a complete blur as it zipped by. At this rate, she was going to get a speeding ticket.

"Just for informational purposes, when was the last time you were in love, Em?"

Hmmm...I'd just ended a relationship with Mark, a lovely professor from the university. He was a great guy but I'd never loved him. Before that was James...a detective with the local police. We'd dated awhile but we'd never hit our stride. So he was also a no. Then there was–

"If it takes you this long to answer then it's been a damn long while."

"It has been," I easily agreed. "I don't go around falling in love easily. It takes time and a truly terrific guy."

"Time? Why does it take time?"

It was my turn to sigh heavily. "We've been through this. I need to get to know a man before I can say that I love him. That doesn't happen overnight."

"Okay, I won't argue that point with you...although I could. Let's talk about you and Owen."

How much longer was this drive? I checked my watched and groaned silently. We still had two hours to go and I was trapped in this car with a trained therapist. There was no escape.

"Fine, let's talk about me and Owen. Want do you want to

know?"

"Now be honest. Do you think about him all the time?"

Did I? I had to admit that I did.

"Quite a bit. Probably more than I should but to be fair you're the one that brought him up when we got in the car."

"Were you already thinking about him while you were waiting for me to pick you up? Did you think about him during your flight?"

Fuck.

"Yes."

"Do you feel happy? A feeling of energy and vibrancy?"

Vibrancy? Christ on a crutch.

"I guess you could say I've had a lot of energy. We didn't get much sleep this weekend but I managed fine."

In fact, I'd glowed but I wasn't about to tell Shelby that.

"Has your appetite changed? Diminished or grown?"

There were times I couldn't stand Shelby. This was one of them.

"I've been eating like a horse but I would think that would be normal. I was very…active over the weekend."

"And the sex was amazing?"

Oh my heavens.

"Yes."

"Are you thinking of you two as a couple? Are you thinking about the future with him in it? Even if it's something as simple as next Friday night. Do you assume that you'll be with him?"

We hadn't talked about our next date but…

"Yes. Is the interrogation over, Officer?"

"One more question. How does he take his coffee?"

"Two sugars. No cream."

"Okay, I lied. One more question. You dated Mark for a couple of months. How did he take his coffee?"

I had no fucking idea.

"I forgot," I replied with a careless shrug. "That was a long time ago."

Shelby laughed as she whipped around a slow car in the left lane. Jesus frog, it was like riding with a racecar driver.

"You and Mark broke up two weeks ago. That doesn't qualify as a long time ago. You have all the signs, Em. I think you might be in love."

No. Just…no.

"It's way too soon to be saying that," I protested. "We just met last week. It's been *less than a week.*"

"Sometimes you just know. You're really into it, far more than any guy in recent memory. Can't you even admit that you might be falling in love with him?"

No.

"It's the first rush of infatuation. You know…sex and all that stuff."

"It could be, or it could be love. You might want to think about it, really dig deep into your emotions. You might be surprised."

I wasn't in love, and all that digging sounded like no fun at all.

"If I say that I'll think about it, can we change the subject?"

"We can change it, no strings attached. I'm just trying to help you but this is really all up to you, Em. If you want me to shut up, all you had to do is say so."

"Shut up."

"Then I will." There was a long pause before she spoke again. "I don't suppose you want to talk about your childhood or how you feel about your mother?"

Absolutely not.

"Just drive, Shel. I'm not here for a therapy session. Why don't we talk about your wedding?"

That was all it took. Shelby was off and running with the topic as her future in-laws were being a pain in the ass about the guest list. Mission accomplished. Now we were concentrating on her. Not me.

Me…who was not in love in the least. Right?

CHAPTER SEVENTEEN

Owen

UNLOCKING THE FRONT door, I placed my suitcase in the foyer and then stepped aside to let my assistant into the house. Carly had picked me up from the airport in Chicago and I'd promised her a glass of wine when we arrived. She was really more like the sister that I'd never had than an assistant. She never held back an opinion, and often times I felt like I worked for her, not the other way around.

"Damn, it's cold out there," I said, shutting the door firmly against the frigid temperatures outside. I already missed the tropical weather in the Caribbean. It was always good to come back from a trip and sleep in your own bed but this time I wasn't looking forward to it. Emmy wouldn't be there. "Come in and get warm. Not that it will be much warmer in here than it was out there. I turned down the thermostat before I left."

"And I turned it up this morning," Carly laughed, shedding her coat and draping it over a kitchen chair. "I also stopped at the grocery store to make sure you had food to make breakfast tomorrow."

"You're an amazingly efficient woman."

Almost as efficient as Emmy.

"Breakfast is the most important meal of the day. Besides, if I hadn't you would have been complaining tomorrow about how you didn't have milk for your coffee."

"I don't take milk in my coffee."

"I'm sure you'll need fresh milk for something. Now how about that wine?"

I poured us each a glass and we settled on the couch in front of the gas fireplace. The flames danced cheerily and my tired body began to relax. It had been a long day of travel. My stomach growled, reminding me that I hadn't eaten since the Miami airport.

"Do you want to order a pizza? Or is Jake expecting you home for dinner?"

Carly took a sip of her cabernet. "Jake and the kids already had dinner. Baked ziti that I prepared this morning. All my husband had to do was heat it up in the oven. Although knowing him, he decided to take them all for burgers. Can we get extra cheese?"

Carly and Jake had been married for almost ten years and had two kids under the age of eight which meant that they were tired a good deal of the time.

"We absolutely can," I replied, picking up my phone to order. "Are you sure Jake will be okay with this?"

"Jake is fine but if you're worried, I'll send him another text. I already let him know that we were here."

"I wouldn't want to get you in trouble."

"Every now and then Mom gets a night off. Picking you up at the airport and sharing a pizza is almost a vacation for me these days."

"You love it."

"I do but the quiet here is just heaven."

Quickly I ordered the pizza – a large with sausage and extra cheese – before retrieving the remote and flipping through the channels.

"How about this cooking show?"

Carly reached for the remote and tossed it against the sofa cushions. "How about you tell me what's going on? And don't lie to me and say you don't know what I mean because you most certainly do know what I mean."

Did I mention that she can read me like a book?

"I really don't know what you mean. Want to give me a hint?"

Carly's brows shot up. "Tell me about her."

Ah. I understood now. I'd mentioned to Carly in one of our business calls that I'd met a woman. It had been in passing when she'd asked me how I was killing time since the wedding was called off.

"*Her* has a name. It's Emerson Grant but everyone calls her Emmy. What do you want to know? Do I need a good lawyer?"

"Ha ha. Very funny. No, you don't need a lawyer unless you're planning to lie to me. You met her on the island?"

"I did, and no, I'm not planning to lie."

"Was she a tourist there? Part of the wedding party?"

"She was the event planner. She lives here in Arborville."

Carly nodded and smoothed down the hem of her sweater. "Okay, her name is Emmy and she's an event planner. What else do you know about her?"

"I know lots of things. Why is this so important to you? You rarely ask me about the women I date."

"Because usually they don't mean anything. But this one does. I can tell by the way you said her name. You face turned all dreamy and distant." Carly sighed and took another sip of wine. "You're in love."

She didn't phrase it as a question. A simple statement but it was loaded with meaning.

"You sound very sure."

"I am. So I want to know more about this woman that turned your head in one measly weekend. She must really be something to do that."

Emmy was that and more.

"I think you'd really like Emmy if you met her. She's smart, funny, down to earth, and well spoken. She owns her own event planning business so you know she's hardworking. Lisa and Dan adore her and she was the only one they wanted to do their wedding."

Images of Emmy when she was pulling the last-minute ceremony together filled my head. She'd been so sweet to Dan and Lisa, not caring if she contracted the bubonic plague. She'd simply wanted to make their wedding as special as possible under the circumstances.

"And you love her."

Did I? It was a good question at this juncture of the relationship. I'd asked it myself a few times last night and again this morning when I'd practically had to wrench myself out of her arms so we could catch our flight. I hadn't seen her for several hours and already I missed her like crazy.

"Let's just say that I'm falling in that direction."

"So it's not terminal yet?"

"Would it be a problem if I was in love?" I asked Carly. "I'm a grown man and I have pretty decent taste in women. She's not a gold digger, if that's what you're thinking."

As an academic, I'd never been flush with cash until the website became popular. In fact, I'd only recently paid off my student loans. Now I had an excellent income but I'd been sensitive to females that might only be attracted to me financially.

"I just don't want you to get hurt." She leaned forward and looked me directly in the eye. "Is she in love, too?"

The million-dollar question. I had no idea.

"I haven't asked her and she hasn't said," I replied honestly. "I'm sure we'll get around to discussing it before long."

As cautious as Emmy had lived her life, she wasn't going to declare her love for me – or anyone – after one weekend. It simply wasn't her style. I'd had a major victory just getting her to admit that our romance wasn't a short-term vacation thing. It was real and we needed to give it a chance.

"In the meantime, I want to meet this paragon of virtue. Invite her to Sunday brunch so we can check her out."

"Why on earth would I subject her to your interrogation methods? You're worse than the CIA. I remember what you did to Jake's sister's boyfriend last year."

Carly had made that poor man's life a misery for an entire meal. Jake's sister never heard from him again. For all we knew, he'd changed his name and left the country. All because Carly had asked him about his political affiliations.

"I'd be nice," Carly said, her tone indignant. "Are you afraid to find out something you don't like?"

"No."

"Then invite her for brunch. It will all be fine."

"Promise me." I shook my finger at Carly. "Promise me you won't go checking her out on the internet or asking her how much money she makes. I mean it, Carly."

"I promise." She stuck out her tongue. "You need to have a little faith in me."

"I'll invite her but I can't promise that she'll be able to go. She works almost every weekend."

"We can make it dinner during the week."

How could I possibly sell this invitation to Emmy?

Hey Emmy, how about having an awkward meal with my assistant and her family while they try to find out if you've killed a man and left him for dead? It's just that they're like family to me.

It was no way to make a woman fall in love with you.

★ ★ ★

I'D UNPACKED MY suitcase and thrown the laundry into the washer, taken a long hot bath, and put on my favorite flannel pajamas with the ratty hem. Now I was lying on the couch with a cup of hot chocolate and Shelby's book, determined to finish it once and for all.

It wasn't that it wasn't interesting and entertaining…it was. It's just that it was hard for me to sit still for too long and read anything. But since I'd consented to be in a real actual relationship with Owen – and I really truly liked him a whole lot – I'd figured that I'd better bone up on what that meant.

Owen wasn't like the other men that I'd dated in the past. He didn't appear to be trying to fool me into doing something I wouldn't normally do – loan him money, have a threesome with his ex, wait on him hand and foot, marry him so he could get a green card.

Yes, all actual dating situations I'd been in. Sad, I know.

He hadn't rushed me into bed, either. If anything, I'd pushed the subject. He genuinely seemed to want to explore our feelings for one another and it was kind of freaking me out. It had been a long time since I'd dated a guy who just...cared about me. Who would that have been?

Trent, maybe? I'd dated him from twenty-eight to thirty. He'd told me he loved me and even talked about marriage. Then he'd become frustrated with the time my business took away from us and he'd pushed me to offload some of the work onto my employees. I'd taken that advice, restoring some well-needed work life balance, but I'd also taken a good look at Trent. He wasn't a huge cheerleader for my career and at one point had even suggested that I might give it up if we had children. I'd ended the relationship after two years. We simply hadn't had the same goals for the future. Last I heard, Trent had married a lovely pediatric nurse.

After Trent, and turning thirty, I'd found the pool of eligible males rather shallow and small. I'd dated a slew of men that I could only describe as *not for me*. Eventually I'd come to the conclusion that while men were nice in small doses, a steady diet of them could make a girl sick to her stomach.

Seeing the couples that came through my event planning

business didn't help the situation, either. Some of them were so sweet and clearly in love and some of them were a nightmare. There were times that the bride and groom could barely stand to be in the same room.

So I guess you could say that I'm cynical as hell.

Shelby's book was the opposite of that. Caution mixed with optimism was how I would describe her advice.

Had I become the female and thirtysomething equivalent of an old man yelling at kids to get off his lawn? I wasn't enjoying the mirror that I was looking into. I didn't want to think I was the type of person that would pass up a great guy because I assumed that there was something wrong with him.

What was wrong with Owen? I hate myself for even asking the question but I had to admit that it was weighing on my mind. He couldn't possibly be this wonderful, right? He had to have flaws. The big question was, were they flaws that I could live with?

Figuratively speaking, of course. I wasn't thinking about us living together this early in the relationship. Slow and steady. That was my motto. No need to rush. If it was mean to be, we'd get there in the end.

Except that Shelby's book, to my surprise, wasn't a huge proponent of taking the slow lane. There was a great deal about how love made everything different and better and how it added to your life. The advice was basically to keep your head on, don't rush in too fast, until – and this was the big part – your guy was all in. And when that happened, it was off to the races.

There was even a chapter about how to know when it's love. As if I wouldn't know. I would know for sure. Who are these poor souls walking around not knowing if they're in love or not? Do they bump into walls, too?

I was going to have to give Shelby my honest opinion about her book. Good. Interesting. It just wasn't a book for me. I didn't need that sort of help. I had it all together.

CHAPTER EIGHTEEN

Emmy

OWEN AND I had set up lunch together the next day. The first day back in the office after time away was always busy, but as he'd pointed out I had to eat at some point. To be honest, I was really missing him. This morning I'd almost poured him a cup of coffee in my kitchen when he'd never even been to my house. I could juggle my schedule for a few hours to fit him in.

I'd showed up to his office ten minutes early which to me is right on time. It was a nondescript brick building in the downtown area of Arborville that I'd walked by a thousand times without noticing. It didn't have a sign or any indicator of what was inside, which might be a good thing. I could imagine it wouldn't be pleasant if a few disgruntled clients pounded on the door, angry after a bad date or two.

The inside had an industrial loft vibe with soaring ceilings, exposed brick and pipes, and highly polished concrete floors. I was ushered to the top floor that was set up as some sort of soundstage or photography studio. Owen was in conversation with an upset older gentleman but the minute I stepped into the room he looked up, our gazes meeting.

For a moment the whole world ceased to exist. That familiar thrill ran up my spine and his smile turned my knees to jelly. Could I really have walked away from him at the end of the weekend?

He said something to the other man and then strode toward me, his arms outstretched. Normally I would have played it cool and that's exactly the message my brain sent my limbs, but they weren't taking orders at the moment. I practically leapt into his arms, despite about a dozen onlookers. I wasn't much for public displays but over twenty-four hours of not seeing him had clearly had an effect.

When he lifted his head from our soul-scorching kiss I was a flustered mess and he was all smug male. Dammit. I didn't like the fact that he knew how strongly he affected me.

"Emmy, I'm so glad you're here," he murmured, placing another soft kiss on my lips. "I wanted to show you around a little before we had lunch. Is that okay?"

Since I couldn't put words together very well, I had no choice but to nod in agreement. I was hungry but I wanted to know more about Owen's company.

"We're filming a social media commercial here today," he said, wrapping an arm around my waist and urging me forward. "We've invited some of our most recently engaged and married couples to give testimonials and they'll all be edited together to make the spot."

There were several people in the large room but now I could see that there were two types, employees and happy in love duos. The former were rushing around and the latter were far more relaxed, sitting on an old sofa and chairs set in the corner.

"You make them here?"

"We do," Owen confirmed. "Our ads have a distinctive look and feel with the couples all dressed casually in front of that black backdrop. Let me introduce you to them."

There were three couples for the commercial, one that looked to be in their twenties, one that looked late thirties or early forties, and then an older couple that might have been in their early sixties. I was terrible at guessing ages but it was easy to see what Owen was going for here. An ad that would illustrate that online dating was for everyone of every age.

"This is Adam and Madison," Owen introduced the young couple first. "Hannah and Frank. And over here we have Will and Theresa. Everyone, this is my girlfriend Emmy. She's an event planner here in Arborville."

His *girlfriend.* I was official. Take that, Shelby.

"Do you do weddings?" Madison piped up. She was a cute blonde with bright blue eyes. "We got engaged recently and we need to plan the wedding but we have no idea what we're doing or even where to start."

I practically rubbed my hands together in glee. This – right here – is what I loved. Helping people have their dream day.

"I do and I'd be happy to help you. If you're not looking for a planner, I can just answer your questions."

I never went into selling mode, though. It wasn't my style. If people wanted to hire me that was great, but I was happy to give away some advice for free.

The man Owen had been talking to when I'd arrived was standing at his elbow, holding a clipboard and looking impatient.

"Honey, can you excuse me for a few minutes?" Owen asked. "It looks like they need me for a quick conference."

"Sure, I'll be fine." I sat down next to Madison since she was the one that had inquired about her wedding. "Let me know when you're done and we'll go to lunch."

"It won't be long," Owen promised and headed over to the camera with the scowling older man. He might be the director but what I knew about filming a commercial could be placed on the head of a pin.

"So Adam and Madison, how long have you been engaged?" I asked, not wanting to sit in silence. I was strangely curious about the couples my *boyfriend* had created with his test and website.

"Just a few months," Adam said, his voice quiet in contrast to his more bubbly fiancee. "But we'd like to get married next Valentine's Day. Is that enough time to plan?"

"It is," I assured them. "What sort of event did you have in mind? Small? Large?"

"Small," Madison said, grabbing Adam's hand with a big grin. "Something intimate and romantic. I don't want a big expensive wedding."

"Wise, especially as I was never a proponent of a young couple going into debt for the big day. Of course, these two might have a massive trust fund for all I knew and money was no object."

"Wish we'd done that," Frank said, the male from the middle couple. His tone was bitter and his expression was the same. "Now we're paying off student loans, car debt, a mortgage, and our wedding."

His significant other Hannah, who had been smiling only minutes before, now looked pissed the hell off.

"It's not my fault," she hissed, tugging her hand away from his. "You wanted the wedding as much as I did."

"I wanted a wedding. I didn't want that circus that we had. Hell, I didn't even know half of the people there."

"Half of those people were my family and friends."

Frank leaned forward, his lips a narrow line. "As long as we're talking about your family, let's talk about your mother–"

"My goodness," Will interrupted loudly, slapping his thighs for emphasis. "Did you hear we're supposed to get more snow on Thursday? I was hoping for spring but I think Old Man Winter has one last hurrah."

"I heard that, too," Theresa said, patting Will's hand. "Brrrr! I'm ready for some warmer weather."

Bless the older couple, they were trying to keep the atmosphere casual and light. Hannah and Frank looked like they wanted to kill each other, though. I'd had couples like this before and it was never about the cost of the wedding. It always went deeper than that. As a rule, I didn't play therapist.

A hand landed on my shoulder and I looked up to see a smiling Owen. "Are you ready to go?"

I was more than ready. It appeared that Owen's test hadn't worked quite as well for at least one couple. What did that say about me and him?

Owen

"WHAT DID YOU think of the office?" I asked Emmy during lunch. I was anxious for her to be impressed, as pathetic as it sounds.

"I didn't realize you had so many people working for you. I sort of pictured a guy on a computer maintaining the website and you in an office working on refining the test." Emmy laughed and my heart lurched at the sound. She was positively gorgeous when she smiled. "Clearly, I was mistaken in more ways than one."

"It takes an entire team of IT people to keep the website up and running while also keeping the data that we store protected from hackers. We also have a large marketing team in addition to the operations department that takes care of all things business related. Plus, I have several psychologists on staff and we constantly work to refine our matching program."

"I didn't realize it was so complicated. I'm impressed. My business looks mighty small compared to yours. I have less than a half dozen employees and some are seasonal."

"I'll bet you have a black book full of contractors," I replied taking a bite of my pulled pork sandwich. We were having lunch at the barbecue joint in between our two offices. "Cake bakers, bands, etc. You probably know every decent place to have a wedding for hundreds of miles."

"As a matter of fact…I do." Her smile faded and she shifted uncomfortably in her chair. "I hate to say this and it may not be any of my business, but one of the couples you had in today wasn't exactly blissful. In fact, they seemed to be at each other's throats."

I hadn't noticed anything, but then I hadn't spent much time talking with the couples today. We'd chosen them through an exhaustive process that included written and in-person interviews.

"I'm sure it was only a tiff. All couples argue. My psychological team chose them and they had to jump through a dozen hoops to be selected."

"You didn't pick them?"

"No, my two assistants did."

That seemed to make her feel better because her entire frame seemed to relax slightly. She'd been tense about mentioning it to me.

"You don't need to worry about talking to me about these things," I assured Emmy. "I value your opinion. Although I admit that today was purely about showing off a little bit."

"I was impressed." Something wasn't quite right. She was fidgeting with her fork now. I waited quietly while she figured out what she wanted to say. "My friends are having a game night this weekend. They've invited us."

I liked the way that sounded. Us. This was no affair. We were a couple.

"That sounds like fun. What kind of games do you usually play?"

"A lot of the classics like Monopoly, Clue, or Trivial Pursuit."

"I always win at Monopoly."

Chuckling, she tapped her chest. "I'll have you know that

I'm the champion among my friends."

"Bring it on," I laughed. "I can't wait for the showdown."

Her smile dropped and she was fidgeting again. "You don't have to go if you don't want to."

"Why wouldn't I want to? Seriously, I love board games."

"I know that it's…early in our…relationship to be meeting the friends."

"Then I probably shouldn't mention that my lead assistant Carly is anxious to meet you. She's the closest thing I have to family. I was going to invite you for Sunday brunch one of these weekends that you don't have to work."

Emmy's skin turned pale and I thought she might fall off of her chair for a moment. She recovered quickly but there was a definite panic in her eyes.

"We can table the discussion for awhile if you want."

"No, it's fine. Meeting my friends is exactly the same as meeting your friends. I bet we love each other's friends. It will all be great. So sure, let me look at my schedule and see if I have any time off. This is a tough time of the year, though."

I'd just learned a little tidbit about Emmy. She rambled when she was nervous. It was cute.

"Just let me know and I'll schedule it. No hurry. Whenever you have the time."

"Do you have brunch with Carly every Sunday?"

"Nope, I'm usually too busy but we try and get together every few months." I reached across the table and laid my hand over Emmy's. "They'll adore you, and I think you'll like them, too."

She shrugged carelessly as if she wasn't worried in the slightest. “It will be fine. Now tell me more about this commercial.”

Emerson Grant wasn’t fooling anyone. She was nervous about the whole *meet the friends* thing.

And the honest truth? I was nervous, too. I was simply better at hiding it.

Because if Friday night didn’t work out, I had a feeling I’d get kicked to the curb pretty fast.

CHAPTER NINETEEN

Emmy

"WHERE'S SHELBY?"

That was the question on everyone's mind this evening but Ashlyn had finally put our worries into words when she'd pulled me into her kitchen.

"I don't know," I replied, setting the pizza boxes out in a row. We were supposed to be getting dinner ready since it had shown up at the door minutes before. "Maybe they forgot about tonight."

Ashlyn shook her head as she placed a stack of silverware next to the plates. "Shelby never forgets anything."

That was true. Although I was playing it cool, I was actually kind of worried myself. I'd sent Shelby a text on Thursday about how much I'd enjoyed her book and I hadn't heard back from her.

That was really strange. Shelby was excellent about keeping in contact.

"When was the last time you talked to her?"

"Wednesday," Ashlyn said. "What about you?"

"Wednesday."

"Nothing since?"

"No, but this is a busy time of year for Shel. I'm sure there's a reasonable explanation."

Ashlyn pulled her phone from her pocket. "I think we should call Mia."

Bad idea. Then we'd have another person all the way across the ocean worrying as well.

"It's the middle of the night in Scotland. We'd scare the hell out of her if we called now and said we hadn't talked to Shelby in a few days."

"And she didn't show up tonight. This has been on our calendars for weeks," Ashlyn said, her expression one of worry. "This isn't like Shelby at all."

"So send her another text. Since she knows that we would worry about her, she's sure to answer this time."

Nodding, Ashlyn tapped out a brief message and hit the send button. "There. Cross your fingers that she replies. In the meantime, can I just say how great your new boyfriend is? Handsome, funny, intelligent, and totally not full of himself. Only you would go to a Caribbean island and come home with a hunk and a half."

"You met yours in an elevator."

"Your story is more romantic."

"Yours is cuter."

They didn't settle the matter because Ashlyn's phone beeped loudly. She held up the screen. Shelby. Thank goodness.

"See? She's fine."

Ashlyn tapped the screen and the text popped up.

I'll talk to you later.

"That's it?" I took the phone from Ashlyn and tried to scroll down but there wasn't anything else. "That's her entire reply?"

"That's it," Ashlyn agreed. "Quite the curt dismissal. I guess Shelby's in the middle of something. Do you think she and Brad are fighting? That would explain why they're not here tonight and also why she doesn't have time to talk to us."

The last time I'd seen Shelby and Brad together they hadn't been all that happy with one another. Brad had been a dick and Shelby had fumed all the way home. Later she'd told them that he'd apologized and they'd made up.

"The closer the wedding gets, the more stress they're going to feel," I replied. I'd seen it played out hundreds of times. "Sometimes they're going to take that stress out on each other. So the answer is yes, I do think they might be arguing. All couples fight, right?"

At least that's what Owen had said at lunch on Tuesday.

"Kyle and I argue every now and then," Ashlyn said. "But not anything terrible. We get mad and then we get over it."

"That's the way to do it. Just don't say anything you can't take back."

Ashlyn glanced down at her phone and grimaced. "Do you think one of them said something like that?"

"Maybe, but she's asking for space so I think we need to give it to her."

"Agreed," my friend sighed, tucking her phone away. "I'm still going to worry a little, though."

"She'd tell you not to, I bet."

In a way it was easier because Shelby wasn't here. I'd assumed she and Owen would go off tonight and talk shop while the rest of us played Clue.

We don't play Trivial Pursuit with Ashlyn's boyfriend Kyle any more. He's a certified genius and kicks all our asses.

"Shelby and Owen have a lot in common."

Ashlyn poured out two margaritas. "Psychology stuff. I'm sure you both have shared interests. Have you been able to spend much time together this week?"

Surprisingly we had, despite having to catch up at work. We'd had dinner together on Wednesday night, lunch on Thursday, and dinner and a movie Friday.

No, we hadn't had sex again yet. We'd both been busy and exhausted with work but I was thinking that tonight might be the time. What was the point of having a regular boyfriend if I didn't get to have sex with him?

"We have. It's not easy, though. We both have crazy schedules. Luckily Owen's is much more flexible than mine."

"A man who compromises for you. Now that's a good one. I think you hit the jackpot this time, Em."

Had I? Sometimes Owen seemed far too good to be true. But I was falling for him anyway.

Help.

★ ★ ★

EMMY WAS A cruel woman, and she knew exactly what she was doing. In fact, it was clear this woman was a master at arousing my most prurient interests and then walking away with nothing but the gentle sway of her hips.

Fuck.

The last thing I needed was for her friends to see me with a raging hard on but it looked like that was probably going to be how the game night was going to go. I could practically hear her friends talking amongst themselves after we left.

Did you see the dick on that guy? He must get hard with a good stiff breeze. Poor Emmy. Do you think she knows he's a pervert?

She'd done it the first time when we were playing Monopoly. I'd just landed on Park Place and had every intention of purchasing the property when I felt her hand on my thigh, rubbing up and down. Not quite all the way to my cock but just brushing her fingertips right below a mere centimeter from my balls.

The way we were sitting at the dining room table with the tablecloth covering everything below our waist no one had any clue what this naughty woman was doing. Like this was any other normal evening, Emmy was chatting and laughing, this time about the weatherman. He liked to dress up in funny costumes. Last night he'd been a rain cloud. Not that I gave a shit right then. The only thing I'd cared about was what her hidden fingers were doing out of everyone's sight. If anyone noticed that I was being uncharacteristically quiet they were too polite to say so.

Then later when the pizza had arrived, she'd brushed against me as I was handing the delivery kid a tip. Her breasts against my back, her hand ghosting over my ass. Really, Emmy? I'd had to quell the urge to throw her over my shoulder and drag her to the nearest horizontal surface. Or vertical. I wasn't fussy.

The third time had been when I'd entered the kitchen to

refill her margarita. I wasn't much for tequila but Kyle had told me that the ladies loved these on game night. Looked like I would need to drag out the blender and learn to make a batch. While placing the pitcher back in the refrigerator, Emmy had come up behind me and ran her hand down my back and then back up again, her short nails scratching straight through my cotton shirt. I'd whirled around but she was already sashaying out of the kitchen, shooting me a smirk over her shoulder.

There was so much more to this woman than what she let the world see, and I loved the fact that she was so open about her needs.

As in...she needs me.

We'd eaten, finished the game – Emmy had won – and settled into the living room to sit in front of the fireplace and talk. Ashlyn was a complete sweetheart, that was obvious. She was a lover of the past and of course I'd been in her store. She had the best vinyl collection in the state.

Her boyfriend Kyle Lewis wasn't anything like I'd expected him to be. I'd thought he might be a cocky know-it-all, smug and basically a pain in the ass. Not in the least. He was clearly a regular guy who liked to watch hockey and drink beer. He didn't brag or even talk about himself much. He also worshipped the ground Ashlyn walked on. They were the cutest couple I'd seen in a long time and I'd seen a bunch this week.

"Emmy tells me you're working on a book, Kyle." I placed my arm around Emmy's shoulders. "When will it be out?"

"I've barely started it. It's really just an idea and a barebones outline at this point. It was Ashlyn's idea, actually. She suggested that since people are always trying to ask me questions maybe I should put some of my thoughts and ideas on paper."

Very slowly and deliberately I began tracing patterns on Emmy's arm, her thin blouse barely any barrier, while continuing my conversation with Kyle. Two could play this game. She shivered and I had to hide my smile of triumph. She was as affected as I was.

Ashlyn lifted the edge of one of the drapes and frowned. "I thought the snow wasn't supposed to start until early morning."

Emmy immediately stood to join Ashlyn at the window. "It's really flying out there."

"We're supposed to get four inches," Ashlyn said. "Maybe you should get on the road now. I don't want you to get stranded anywhere."

Emmy was already nodding in agreement. "I think that's a good idea. Owen, what do you think?"

I thought it was a great idea, too.

Emmy was going to get much more than four inches tonight.

CHAPTER TWENTY

Emmy

OWEN DIDN'T SAY much during the drive back to my place, his attention on the snow-covered roads. When we arrived, he followed me into the house just as quietly with his arm around me so I wouldn't slip and fall on the front porch steps. I locked the door behind us and quickly shed my coat, hanging it on a set of hooks in the foyer.

"Kick your shoes off and make yourself at home. How about a glass of wine?" I asked, making a beeline for the kitchen. "Or maybe a brandy? It will warm us up. The temperature really dropped in the last few hours."

According to the weather report, this was supposed to be winter's last hurrah and warmer weather would be just around the corner. More specifically in only two days.

Standing on my tiptoes, I reached up into the top shelf of the cabinet and retrieved the bottle of brandy that I rarely used. In my day to day life there simply wasn't a great deal of occasions that called for it. Normally the girls and I drank margaritas or cosmopolitans. In the summer, I'd make pitchers of sangria and we'd drink them out on the back patio. But cold winter nights and fireplaces were practically invented for brandy. All we needed was a cuddly Saint Bernard to bring it to us.

"I'll just grab a couple of glass–"

When I'd turned around, I was surprised to see Owen standing right behind me. Close.

"You're really quiet when you want to be," I said breathlessly. "I didn't hear you at all."

"I took my shoes off." Owen pointed to his sock clad feet and then plucked the brandy bottle from my hand, setting it down on the counter. "I think we have some unfinished business first, though."

Owen was a tall man with long limbs and his body crowded me back against the kitchen cabinets. This close, I could feel the heat from his skin penetrate even my denim jeans and sweater. The temperature in the room had just ratcheted up about twenty or thirty degrees.

"Unfinished business?" I echoed, leaning my torso backward to look up into his face. I wasn't a petite little flower but he still towered over me by at least six inches or more. "I'm not sure what you mean."

But I was beginning to. I'd done a little bit of teasing at game night and I had a feeling it was going to pay off. Lucky me. Normally I was much more direct but I thought this might be more fun.

"You wanted my attention. Now you have it. All of it."

I certainly did. His gaze was laser focused on me, raking me from head to toe. From the desire in his eyes, he liked what he was seeing.

My nipples peaked under my bra, rubbing against the lace and sending arrows of arousal straight to my lower belly. The blood had begun to roar in my ears like a freight train and I had to grab onto his shoulders not to end up in a heap on the floor. Decadent images of ripping his shirt off of his body ran through my brain.

"Do you know what you were doing to me tonight?" he asked, his arms snaking around my waist and pulling me closer. "You were driving me crazy."

"That was the plan," I admitted, our lips crashing together. His tongue demanded entry and I didn't deny him. His hands drifted down to my hips and the next thing I knew I was being lifted up onto the kitchen counter. "Owen, what are you doing?"

Tugging at his belt, he gave me a slow, evil smile. "Fucking you, of course. That's what this has all been about, right?"

No. Well...yes.

"You haven't wanted to all week. What changed your mind?"

His fingers stilled just as he finished pulling down his zipper. "Is that what's been going on in that pretty head of yours? You think I don't want you? Honey, I want you any way that I can get you, all the fucking time. I was just giving you some space this week. Trying to be a damn gentleman."

A gentleman. Taking a moment to digest that comment, I decided it sounded awful.

"Don't do that ever again."

He ripped his shirt over his head and tossed it away onto the tile floor. That wide chest was bared for my inspection, both visual and manual. Yum. "I won't. Now let's get you naked. Or at least naked enough."

For a moment I opened my mouth to object but then I remembered that this was what I'd been wanting all week. The fact that the kitchen counter wasn't the most comfortable location wasn't really the point. I'd wanted him to fuck me and now he was ready to do it. With any lucky we'd do it here and then go into the bedroom and do it all over again.

Apparently, I didn't move fast enough because Owen was shoving my sweater up to my armpits and pulling my bra cups down, exposing my breasts to the cool air. The nipples were already hard as nails and he brushed them a few times with his thumbs before bending his head and sucking them into his warm mouth. Scraping the sides with his teeth, he ran his tongue around in circles before pulling off with a pop and shifting his attention to the other side.

My fingers tangled in his hair and my nails dug into his scalp as his mouth worked black magic, building my arousal until I was ready to explode. A sheen of sweat now covered my skin, although the kitchen was chilly. Having a mind of their own, my legs had wrapped themselves around his waist, anchoring him close in case he had any ideas about making a break for it before we were through.

His hard cock was pressed against my center and I swear it was as hot as an oven. Grinding against him, I tried to get just the right friction I needed to send me over. My breath was coming in pants and gasps as I teetered on the edge.

Placing a strong arm under my bottom, he slipped my jeans and panties down my legs and off, leaving me bare-ass naked on the cool granite. It did nothing to lower my temperature.

"Are you ready, honey?" Owen crooned in my ear as he tugged at the waistband of his jeans, pulling them down along with his boxers so his cock sprang free. "I can't wait to be inside you."

I'd been so lost to the pleasure that I didn't realize that at some point he'd dug into his pocket for a condom. He tore open the packet with his teeth and then rolled it on with my help, which may have been more of a hindrance considering how much my fingers were shaking. I needed him now.

"Now," I whispered, my head falling back so his mouth could find the pulse at the base of my neck. "Please."

Owen didn't make me wait a second longer, thrusting inside of me all the way to the hilt. We both groaned as he bottomed out, our breaths mingling together as his lips captured mine in a sloppy, wet kiss. Stretched and full, I wrapped my legs around his middle.

His strokes were slow and deliberate at first but that wasn't what I needed. The pent-up frustration from the week called for something far more…insistent.

I dug my fingers into the muscles of his shoulders. "Fuck me harder. Faster."

Without a word Owen pulled out, wringing a mewl of protest from me but then he placed my legs over his shoulders, opening me as wide as I could go. He set a punishing pace, riding me hard and fast, beads of sweat forming on his forehead.

With every stroke my head smacked into the cabinet behind me and if I didn't come soon I was going to have a concussion, but it never once occurred to me to ask him to stop or be more gentle. If anything, I wanted it rougher. I whispered dirty suggestions into his ear, begging him to fuck me until we both exploded.

Then we both exploded.

Not all at once, though. With each stroke his groin hit my clit, sending me closer to nirvana and when we were both sweaty and barely breathing, he snapped his hips forward, hitting every spot inside and outside just right.

Lights danced behind my lids and my entire body bowed with pleasure as my toes curled inside of my socks. Owen went over right after me, my name on his lips and it sounded sweeter than any endearment I'd ever heard before.

When we both came down from our high, we were officially a mess. My clothes were askew and what was left of my makeup probably made me look like a scary clown from that movie *It*. Owen, however, looked beautiful. His damp skin glowed and his chest rose and fell in time with my own. My fingers had made a mess out of his hair but it only served to give him a rakish air that had me wanting to drag him into the bedroom and continue where we'd left off.

Just as soon as I could breathe again.

★ ★ ★

THE DELICIOUS AROMA of bacon roused me from a deep sleep but it had to simply be a vivid as hell dream, because I didn't have any bacon in the house, nor was I vertical to fry it. Groaning, I opened my eyes and pushed myself up to a sitting position, yawning and stretching my limbs. I was slightly sore in my intimate areas after last night but it wasn't unpleasant, and it was a strong reminder of how Owen and I had gone after each other like animals.

Roar.

Sniffing the air again, the scent of bacon was definitely there. I wasn't dreaming or imagining it. I could also smell the glorious aroma of coffee. The amazing elixir that I needed the most in the mornings. Throwing my legs over the side of the bed, I made a grab for my robe to cover up my naked body. If there was a thief in my house frying bacon and fixing coffee, I didn't want him to see me without clothes.

My stiff legs carried me into the kitchen where the most wonderful sight greeted me. Owen – completely dressed and looking way too handsome for this hour in the morning – was standing at my stove cooking while whistling a happy tune. Dammit, I hated people who whistled in the morning. It was so…carefree. I had a hell of a lot to worry about in the precious time before I left for work.

"I didn't have any bacon."

That's all my sluggish brain could come up with before my coffee. But it was true.

Turning, Owen held out his arm, a big grin on his face. "Emmy, I hope you're hungry. Breakfast is ready."

As if to punctuate his words, the toaster popped up four pieces of perfectly golden toast. I had to admit that Owen's timing was impeccable.

"I didn't have any bacon," I repeated, reaching into the cabinet above the coffee maker. I needed caffeine as quickly as possible.

"I ran to the store," Owen explained, flipping scrambled eggs and bacon onto a plate. "Frankly, there wasn't enough food in that refrigerator to keep a mouse alive, honey."

"I eat out a lot."

And I hated the grocery store. The last time I was there some person ran their cart up on my heel. I limped for three days.

Owen sat my plate down at the little breakfast table and handed me a fork. "Eat up while it's hot."

It was delicious. Even the coffee tasted better than when I made it.

He sat across from me and dug into his eggs, which had cheese, by the way. Eggs and cheese weren't in my refrigerator either. But they were tasty. Did he add garlic and oregano, too?

"You went to the store?"

The caffeine was beginning to kick in nicely and the events around me were starting to make more sense. Owen had gone shopping. Holy shit.

"I did. I just picked up a few staples like bread and milk in addition to bacon and eggs. I did notice that you had peanut butter but nothing to put it on."

That's because I usually just ate it directly from the jar with a spoon. Or my finger. But no double dipping. I have standards.

"Thank you, that's very thoughtful." I glanced at the clock on the wall which read seven-thirty.

"The grocery store is open this early?"

Owen gave me an amused smile. "I went to the twenty-four-hour market a few blocks away."

"Hessell's? I had no idea it was open all the time."

It was probably a new thing they were trying.

But still…my shiny new boyfriend went to the grocery store at o-dark-early and then came back and cooked me breakfast. Pretty damn awesome.

Wait…had he cleaned the counter with some type of disinfectant? I wasn't a total germaphobe but my bare ass had been there mere hours before.

"I wanted to make sure that you had a decent meal before you went off to work. I assume someone, somewhere is getting married today?"

"They are," I confirmed, taking the last bite of my bacon. I could eat like this every day if I had someone to make it for me. "A wedding at two o'clock and then the reception at the Shriner's Hall. They hired an Abba tribute band as the entertainment."

"So you'll be dancing the night away, then?"

Shaking my head, I chuckled at the thought. "Hardly. The reception is right after the ceremony and they only rented the hall until eight. I should be home at a decent hour."

Will you be here?

I didn't ask the question out loud and it sort of hung in the air between us.

"If you're up for some company just let me know," Owen said, popping the last bite of toast into his mouth. "I can bring over some takeout for dinner and we can just relax, but if you're too tired that's fine, too."

It was? He'd made it sound so casual and *whatever*. Did he want to see me tonight or not? I realized that I wanted to see him. A lot. And it didn't have anything to do with his cooking. I just liked being with him.

"I'll send you a text," I promised. "It really just depends on how everything goes. If it's smooth sailing I'll have plenty of energy. If not, then all I'll want is a hot bath and a glass of wine."

Owen smiled and stood to clear the table. "If you like I can probably do a back rub in addition to the takeout dinner."

That wouldn't suck. A sexy man, a hot meal, and a back rub. Far better than anything I'd normally be doing, which was eating peanut butter from the jar and drinking Chardonnay while wearing my rattiest flannel pajamas.

"Careful, I may take you up on that."

"I hope you do." He placed the plates in the sink and then crooked his finger in a beckoning motion. "Now how about my good morning kiss?"

How could I have forgotten to kiss him? Right…caffeine deficit.

I moved to his side swiftly and let him wrap me in his strong arms. This was totally worth getting out of bed for. Our kiss was leisurely but sweet, despite the morning breath. I could get used to this. When he lifted his head, I was a breathless mess.

"I need– I need to start getting ready or I'll be late."

And I sounded breathless, too. Way to be obvious.

"I'll just put the dishes in the dishwasher while you take a shower. Then I'll head out and get out of your hair."

"What are you going to do today?"

"Maybe go for a run and then there's always paperwork. Call me later."

"I will." Hesitating for only a moment, I ran my hands up his chest and around his neck. "I don't suppose there's any way I can convince you to share the shower with me. I need someone to wash my back."

His grin was pure sin. "Sounds like a good plan. Save water

and all that."

We hooked our arms together but he paused and tossed a glance over his shoulder toward the stove and cabinets.

"And by the way, honey, I saw you looking over there earlier. I did clean the countertop. Completely sanitized."

The man was freakin' perfect. Why did that make me so nervous?

CHAPTER TWENTY-ONE

Owen

I FELT A little guilty that Emmy had to work all day while I puttered around for the most part. After my run, I'd stopped at the grocery store to refill my refrigerator and pantry after realizing that I didn't have much more food than Emmy did. Then I'd tried to concentrate on some paperwork but had ended up watching a movie instead, but halfway through fell asleep on the couch. By the time she'd texted me, I'd had a damn good nap and was raring to go for the evening.

I'd thought she might be too tired to see me, but to my surprise she was on board for another night together. We'd spent as much time as possible together since coming back from the island and while I was enjoying it very much, I wasn't sure how Emmy was handling it. She'd been honest from the beginning that she didn't do relationships well as she was so focused on her work. I sure as shit didn't want to become *that guy* who was always hanging around and clinging, making her want to peel me off like a vine.

When I showed up at her house with a bag of Chinese take-out though, I was shocked to see just how exhausted she looked. Her hair was scraped up into a messy bun on top of her head and there were dark circles under her eyes. She must have already had that hot bath she'd talked about because her skin was pink and she smelled of vanilla and coconut. Wearing a pair of sweats and an oversized t-shirt, she looked beautiful but far too fragile for my liking. What she needed was someone to take care of her every now and then. Nothing over the top. Just a hot meal and a shoulder rub. I kind of hoped she might return the favor someday.

She threw up her hands when I walked in and rolled her eyes. "Sorry, I'm such a frump. I couldn't help myself after my bath. I thought about getting dressed again but I found myself pulling on these old things."

Leaning down, I dropped a kiss on her lips. Sweet. "It's fine. I like that you feel comfortable enough to let your hair down…metaphorically speaking."

Sniffing at the air, she reached for the paper bag. "Chinese? That sounds delicious. I'm starving."

I let her take the bag and followed her into the kitchen. "Don't they feed you at these fancy shindigs?"

She wrinkled her nose as she pulled two plates from the cabinet. "I rarely have time to actually eat a meal. I usually make do with a few canapés and some cake. They had a lemon cake and it was delicious."

"That's all you had to eat all day?" I marveled. "It's a wonder that you don't pass out on the job."

"I have a strong constitution." She held up two forks. "Are you ready to eat?"

I was hungry too, although not as much as she was. We sat at her tiny breakfast table and chatted while we ate. She told me about the couple that had tied the knot today and I told her about my day and then the movie that I'd fallen asleep while watching.

"You should finish it," she urged. "It's quite good. You must have been tired to fall asleep."

I waggled my eyebrows and grinned. "*Someone* kept me up last night."

"*Someone* could have stayed in bed instead of running around town buying bacon and eggs."

"And then what would have eaten for breakfast?"

"Peanut butter," she answered immediately. "It's good for you. Lots of protein."

"I'll pass. Do you ever cook for yourself? Even your pots and pans looked pristine. Like they were only there for show and not actual use."

She placed her fork on the edge of her plate and wiped her hands on one of the paper napkins. "I can see we've come to this portion of the relationship where I admit that I can barely cook. I can make a few things under close supervision but on my own I can barely boil water."

Her admission surprised me. She was so competent at everything that it was weird that she couldn't cook for herself.

"I bet you can cook but you just don't like to."

"You would lose that bet. I've cooked in the past but it's about one rung above salmonella poisoning. There is one thing I can make, though. Bread. My grandma taught me."

Picturing Emmy elbow deep in flour made me smile. "Will you make me bread one of these days?"

"Since you made me breakfast…sure. But I usually do it on

one of my days off. It takes a long time."

"I'm worth it."

"You're certainly filled with self-confidence," she teased. "I guess you are worth it."

It was good to see that we could agree on it.

"How about I clean this food up and put the leftovers away, and then we curl up on the couch and I'll give you that back rub that I promised you?"

Honestly, it was going to be as pleasurable for me as it would be for her.

"That sounds–"

Emmy's phone vibrated in the pocket of her sweatpants, interrupting what would surely have been an affirmative answer. Scowling, she read her message, a rather long one since she had to scroll down to finish it.

"I think I'm going to have to take a rain check on that back rub, although I wish I didn't."

I didn't like the worried expression on her face. Now I was concerned as well.

"What's going on? Has something happened?"

"Maybe." She tapped out an answer to the sender. "Ashlyn says she hasn't been able to get Shelby all day long. Neither one of us have actually spoken to her since Wednesday."

"That's unusual?"

"We've gone longer but there's usually a good reason. The last we heard she sent Ashlyn a text last night that said she'd talk to her later. Now it's later and we can't get her at all. Ashlyn's tried her cell phone, her land line, a direct message on Instagram. Heck, she's even tweeted her. Nothing. She wants us to go over to Shelby's house and check on her. She might be sick or hurt."

"I'll go with you," I offered, sweeping up an armful of food to pack away. "Give me five minutes."

Emmy was already shaking her head no. "Thank you, but you don't have to do that. We'll just make a quick run over there and check on her. Hopefully she just needs chicken soup for a bad cold or something. She might even be working on her book and lost track of time."

"Are you sure?" I didn't want to send Emmy out into the cold. "I can drive you there."

"Ashlyn's coming to pick me up. Really, it's okay." She wrapped her arms around me. "It's sweet that you offered to go, though. I do appreciate it but this shouldn't take long."

I hated to ask the next question but I couldn't stop myself.

"Should I stay and wait?"

She hesitated before shaking her head. "I don't want to ask you to do that."

"I don't mind. It's not a big deal."

"I don't know how long I'll be."

"You said that it shouldn't take long," I reminded her, taking a step away from her to toss the empty cartons in the trash.

"It shouldn't but what if it does?" she replied, tapping her chin. "I'm really sorry about this, Owen. I feel terrible that I'm bailing on our plans."

"I feel terrible that you have to go back out tonight." I cupped her chin and leaned down to press a soft kiss on her full lips. "You need your sleep, honey."

It was my own statement that made up my mind. She needed a good night's rest in her own bed. Preferably without me in it.

"I can sleep in tomorrow," she said. "I guess I should put some socks and shoes on. Did I say that I'm sorry yet? Because I am."

"Yes, you did so you don't have to say it again. We'll have another night for your backrub."

If I had my way, we'd have many, many more.

★ ★ ★

Emmy

ASHLYN AND I could hear the heavy beat of music from Shelby's front lawn. Our friend had it cranked into ear-busting territory. She couldn't be having a party because we were the only vehicle in her driveway. Were she and Brad having some sort of *private* party?

Ewww.

I was concerned about Shelby but the last thing I needed was to barge in on some major freaky-deaky time between a soon-to-be married couple. I didn't know much of anything about her love life and frankly, I wanted to keep it that way. We all knew the bare bones… Was it good or was it bad? But if anyone wanted to dress up like Little Bo Peep and get shagged, they weren't admitting it to our little friend group.

Thank goodness.

My finger hovered above the doorbell. We had a key for emergencies but if Shelby was inside, we thought we should ring first. "Maybe this isn't the best idea we've ever had. She could be doing anything in there."

Ashlyn was chewing on her bottom lip and looking unsure as well. "Aren't you worried?"

"I am, but… Shit, what if they're having wild monkey sex in there? Do you want to witness that? Because I sure as hell don't."

"That's why I'm not using my key," she replied, her chin lifting in resolution. "She's our friend and we're worried about her. If she's dressed in leather and carrying a riding crop, we'll apologize and get the hell out of here. I'll buy the brain bleach."

"There isn't enough brain bleach in the world to get rid of that image but okay, here we go."

I pressed the doorbell and we waited. I couldn't hear anything from inside the house except the overly loud music. No movement. No one yelling that they'd be there in a moment.

"She has to be there," Ashlyn muttered, reaching across me to press the bell again. Several times. "She would never leave her music on that loud and not be home."

My stomach was doing that warning thing again, tightening up and telling me that something here was not good.

"I have a feeling she is here and she's…busy," I said, taking a step backward. "If we leave now, they may never know we were here."

Shelby and Brad were inside that house having sex and that's why she'd been ignoring us. She was getting her freak on.

"You don't know that. She could be in there dead."

"Then she isn't going to be answering the door, Ash."

Digging in her purse, Ashlyn pulled out a small keyring with a little pink bow attached to it. I knew it well because I had one just like it, only the bow was red. Shelby's housekey.

"You're going in."

"Nope, *we're* going in. Together. If we interrupt an intimate moment, well...she should have called us back. You know she'd do the same exact thing to us and then spend thirty minutes telling us how it was our own fault."

Shelby would do that. Fuck yes, let's do this.

Ashlyn slipped the key into the lock and turned it to the right. We heard the click and then the door swung open.

No one. The living room and foyer were deserted. Ashlyn strode in and headed straight for the music dock, flipping it off. Then she pointed to an item on the coffee table.

"Shelby's bag is here so she has to be."

Shelby carried around this huge designer leather bag, and her sister Mia always compared it to the Mary Poppins purse where the inside was far larger than the outside. If it was here, so was Shelby. She never went anywhere without it.

"I'll check the kitchen."

Because I didn't want to check the bedrooms. No sirree, I did not. I didn't hear any moaning or sex noises now that the music was turned off, but maybe they were taking a break.

When I first stepped into the kitchen it looked empty as well, but then my gaze skittered over to the sliding glass door area and that's when I saw a pair of legs. More specifically a pair of legs clad in Shelby's black yoga pants with the bright yellow stripe down the side. My heart began to pound and I broke out into a cold sweat when those legs didn't move. Our worst fears had been realized. Shelby was dead. How long had she been like this?

Clutching my chest and reminding myself to breathe, I walked around the kitchen island and found our best friend slumped against the sliding glass doors, her head pillowed on the trash can.

She was cradling an almost empty liquor bottle. Was she…?

"Shelby!" I yelled at the top of my lungs while somehow simultaneously holding my breath. "Wake up!"

Please let her wake up. Please let her wake up.

For a moment she didn't move and I was sure she was dead. But then her body jerked and one eyelid opened slightly. Grabbing onto the kitchen counter, my body sagged in relief. My knees were wobbly and there were spots in front of my eyes. Dear heavens, Shelby was alive and we–

Shelby was alive.

"In here, Ashlyn!"

I wasn't sure what to do. I'd never seen Shelby in this sort of state before. Sure, we'd all had a little too much every now and then but nothing like this. The only thing we'd ever hugged was the toilet when it all came back up.

But I'm practical and efficient.

Kneeling down on the floor next to her, I reached for the bottle but Shelby's grip tightened.

"Hey Shel, how about handing over the hooch? I think you've probably had enough."

Ashlyn's shoes came into my line of vision. "What in the ever-loving hell?"

"She's three sheets to the wind," I announced loudly, getting the reaction that I had hoped for. Shelby's eyes fluttered open again and she yawned loudly, sending the aroma of booze straight into my face. *Lovely. Thanks, Shel.* "She's going to need some water. If she drank all of this she's got to be dehydrated."

"Leave me alone," Shelby muttered, hugging the bottle more tightly to her chest. "Go away. I said I'd call you."

"But you didn't," Ashlyn replied crisply, snagging a plastic sports cup from the upper cabinet. Good thinking. I wouldn't trust Shelby with glass right now, either. "And we got worried, rightly so from the looks of things. Why are you drunk?"

Scowling, Shelby's eyes opened completely this time. "I'm not drunk."

"Then you're doing an amazing impression of it. You should get an Oscar," I replied.

"I'm not drunk."

Shelby's voice had risen but she grimaced at the decibel level of her own voice.

"If you're not drunk, can you explain why you're sitting on the tile floor holding a whisky bottle and smelling like a distillery?"

Her brows pulled together, Shelby appeared to be contemplating my question. "I was drinking earlier and I got hungry."

My gaze flickered over to Ashlyn who shrugged at the cryptic answer.

"And?" I prompted. "You got hungry and…?"

Shelby nodded. "I remembered there was a chocolate donut in the trash can so I came over here to get it. I must have fallen asleep."

I though Ashlyn was going to pass out. I was pretty green myself.

"You were going to eat out of the trash?" Ashlyn asked in a scandalized tone. "Oh my God, Shelby. Are you broke? We would have given you money."

I simply could not imagine Shelby broke. She was very careful with her money and she never seemed to have any financial issues. Did she have a gambling problem, perhaps?

"It's my trash," Shelby muttered, trying to sit up and doing a terrible job of it. "It's not gross if it's your own garbage. I didn't have any other food in the house."

"You could have ordered food," Ashlyn pointed out.

"I just wanted the chocolate. It was my trash."

She had a point but it still turned my stomach. However, now that she wasn't curled into such a tight ball I could get a better look at her.

Shelby looked like hell. I could safely say that I'd never seen her look this bad in the entire time I'd known her. She was always so stylish and neat, but today it looked like she'd been run through a wood chipper and then pieced back together by a five-year-old.

Her auburn hair was a rat's nest on top of her head. There was a pencil stuck in the bun and I wondered if she even remembered that. Her skin was pale to the point that I could see every single freckle on her face. Her eyes were bloodshot, red-rimmed, and glassy, the lids puffy as if she'd been crying for hours. Her shirt had a few stains on it, hopefully not from the donut.

Clearly, she was still drunk and in the middle of sleeping it off when we arrived. Reasoning with her probably wouldn't work. So what did I do?

I tried to reason with her. I didn't know anything else.

"Shelby, you've been drinking. We need to get you up off the floor. Will you let us help you?"

"I don't care."

"You don't care if we help or you don't care if you move?" Ashlyn asked, kneeling down next to us.

"I don't care if I move." Shelby frowned and then unscrewed the lid on the bottle in preparation to take another drink. Oh no. I wasn't going to let that happen. Reaching for the bottle, I managed to pry it out of her fingers. It wasn't easy. She was stronger than she looked.

"I needed that."

"I think you've had enough."

Standing, I placed the bottle on the counter and grabbed the cup of water.

"How about you drink this instead? It's good for you."

Shelby wrinkled her nose but did as I asked, which was a relief because I wasn't sure I would win an argument with a drunk woman. When the glass was half-empty she handed it back to me. What a metaphor for this situation.

"Shelby, why are you drunk?" Ashlyn asked. "What's going on? Where's Brad?"

Slumping back against the sliding glass door, Shelby's eyes welled up with tears.

"He's in Las Vegas."

Las Vegas? I didn't realize his bachelor party was this weekend. Was Shelby trying to match him drink for drink?

"When is he coming back?" I asked. We needed to get her sober and cleaned up before he walked through the door. I was absolutely sure he'd never seen her like this.

"He's never coming back. He went to Las Vegas with his assistant."

Never? That was a damn long time.

"What are you talking about?" Ashlyn said, wrapping her arms around Shelby's waist to try and lever her up off the floor. I grabbed her under the arms and reminded myself to lift with my legs. "Of course, he's coming back."

Shelby shook her head as we lifted her halfway up. Just a foot to go. "He's not. He and Kimberly got married last night."

Married? What in the fuck? I almost lost my grip and dropped Shelby, but somehow Ashlyn and I managed to get her into a standing position.

Now what?

CHAPTER TWENTY-TWO

Emmy

IT TOOK A hot shower and several cups of coffee to sober Shelby up enough to make any sort of sense. Ashlyn had fixed some toast and was now urging her to eat it.

"It will soak up the alcohol in your stomach," Ashlyn explained patiently. "So be a love and just try to eat some of it. And drink this water, too. Caffeine is a diuretic."

"If I eat anything, I'll be sick," Shelby protested, pushing the saucer farther away. We were all sitting on the couch, Ashlyn on one side and me on the other. "My stomach is not a happy camper."

Lifting the whisky bottle from its spot on the table, I held it up for Shelby's inspection. "I would imagine it's not. Was this brand new?"

Shelby rubbed at her temples where I imagined a mariachi band was currently playing their greatest hits. "Sort of. I think Brad had poured himself one drink from it."

"You could have got soused on half this amount," I said, placing the bottle back down. "Now let's go through this again, okay? Where is Brad?"

"I told you. Las Vegas," Shelby said with a loud sigh. "I'm

not making this up."

"We don't think you are," Ashley replied, patting her on the shoulder. "We just aren't clear on all of the details."

"And he went there with his assistant Kimberly?" I asked. "For a business trip or specifically to get married?"

Maybe Brad and Kimberly had a little too much to drink and ended up getting married as a joke.

"To get married, I guess," she shrugged. "At that point in the conversation I didn't really give a fuck about the minute details. If you know what I mean."

I did, but they were kind of important now.

"So you talked to him?" Ashlyn prompted. "What did he exactly say?"

Shelby was rubbing her temples again but I had a feeling that this time it was our fault.

"Of course, I talked to him. He came here to get his suitcase after work on Friday. That's when he told me that he'd fallen in love with Kim and they were flying off to get married. He said he was sorry."

"Sorry?" Ashlyn said, wide-eyed. "The little prick is sorry? Well…it's all okay, then. I didn't realize he was *sorry*."

"If I ever see Brad again in Arborville, even just walking down the sidewalk, I'm going to dick punch him so hard his grandchildren will feel it," I vowed. "Did he say anything else?"

Shelby shrugged. "He said a bunch of things about how we hadn't been truly happy for a long time and it would be a mistake to get married. How she makes him feel young and active again and how they worship each other. Oh, and he said that he always wore a condom so I don't need to go get tested or anything. He said it like he'd done me a big favor. Son of a fucking bitch. I should have smacked him in the head with his cell phone."

Thank heavens for small favors. Shelby could be looking at an STD along with a philandering fiancé.

"That's something…I guess," I replied awkwardly. "Does his family know? Not about the condom thing but about Kimberly."

If you look up the word *snooty* in the dictionary, you'll see a photo of Brad's family. They were proud of it, too.

"He said he would tell them when he got back. They're going to be livid. They don't think anyone is good enough for him and then to elope? His mother is going to take to her bed and maybe never get out of it."

Holy crap on a cracker, Shelby and Brad had been together forever. *Years.* I'll admit that I wasn't Brad's biggest fan but they'd seemed happy. If this could happen to Shelby of all people, no one was safe from having the rug pulled out from under them. No one.

Certainly not me.

But this current situation wasn't about me. This was about Shelby and her terrible, no good man who had absconded to Vegas, leaving her with a broken heart.

"Do you know for sure that they got married last night?" Ashlyn asked. "Brad might have come to his senses by now."

Shelby's lips firmed into a thin line. "I wouldn't take him back if he was the last man on earth. Not if he begged me on his hands and knees wearing a dog collar."

That was an image I didn't need.

"But I know that they did get married," Shelby continued. "Because I'm in a Facebook group with a bunch of his friends and they were all talking about it. There were even photos they shared from Brad's account."

"That was insensitive," Ashlyn sniffed disdainfully. "With friends like that, who needs enemies?"

"I think they'd forgotten that I was a member," Shelby explained. "But yeah, it's still a shitty thing to do. They were all happy for him and no one asked about me."

The last part was said with a sob, and I wrapped my arm around her shaking shoulders as she went on a crying jag that she wholeheartedly deserved. I might even give her back the rest of the whiskey bottle. In fact, I might go out and buy her some tequila and limes to go with it. My friend had a damn good reason to drink and feel sorry for herself.

"I wonder what he told them about the end of your relationship," Ashlyn said out loud. "I bet he blamed you. What a pussy."

I shook my head. "Don't call him a pussy. Pussies are strong. Call him a ball sac. Those things can't take a hit for shit."

"He's a ball sac," Ashlyn declared. "A shriveled-up ball sac."

I gave Shelby a little shake. "And you can do a hell of a lot better than a ball sac. Aren't you glad that you found out what a little douchebag he was now instead of after the wedding?"

Shelby buried her head in hands and groaned. "Oh my God, I'm going to have to explain to three hundred people what happened and everyone one of them will feel sorry for me. The old maid left at the altar."

I didn't want to minimize what Shelby was going through

but I'd actually had a few couples that were *literally* left at the altar. This sucked, but if he hadn't shown up at the church while she was in a white gown and veil that would have been much worse.

"It's none of their business why the wedding is cancelled," I said firmly. "I have an electronic guest list and we can send out a small note that simply says that the nuptials are cancelled and any gifts will be returned. If anyone is gauche enough to ask questions, they'll get the answers they deserve."

More groans from Shelby. "The gifts, the flowers, the cake, the band. It will all have to be cancelled."

"I'll take care of it. You don't need to worry about a thing. That's what I'm here for. This isn't my first rodeo. I've got your back."

This was my specialty. Organization. Putting out fires. Dealing with crying brides.

"I want to hate him," Shelby murmured. "But I don't."

"Really?" Ashlyn drawled, rolling her eyes. "I'll give you some of mine because I hate him enough for all three of us. I always knew he was a loser."

With a quick indrawn breath, she smacked her hand over her mouth. She'd said too much. We'd all decided long ago never to tell Shelby that we didn't like Brad. But in the heat of the moment, the truth had come tumbling out.

Shelby's gaze darted back and forth between Ashlyn and me, understanding dawning on her eyes. "You never liked Brad. Why didn't you say something? All this time I thought you liked him."

"Because it was none of our business," I replied crisply.

"None at all. If you were happy, then we were happy."

"I'm not happy now," Shelby declared. "So are you happy that you were right?"

"No," Ashlyn said instantly. "We never wanted to be right. Ever. Put that out of your mind."

Shelby fell back against the overstuffed cushions of the couch. "How does Mia feel about Brad?"

We were not going there. "You need to ask Mia, but honestly, does it really matter now? You need to stop thinking about him and put yourself first."

"Put myself first," she repeated. "I don't remember the last time I did that."

"Then it should feel great to do it," I said. "For example, name something that you didn't get to do because of Brad."

"One thing? Fuck, I could name a dozen. Follow me."

Shelby hopped up from the sofa and marched toward the bedroom. Ashlyn and I exchanged a worried look but stood and followed. If it made our friend feel better then we'd listen to her all night long.

★ ★ ★

Owen

BACK AT MY own place, I took a quick shower and pulled on a pair of sweatpants and a t-shirt before padding downstairs in bare feet to grab a beer. I was bummed about my evening with Emmy being interrupted but I was also worried about Shelby. I'd known her for several years – albeit casually – and she wasn't the type to fall off the earth and not return her calls.

I was settling down in bed to watch some television when my phone rang. Dan, of all people. I hadn't expected to hear from him for awhile.

"Hey, man. How are you doing?"

"We're doing better," Dan laughed. "All healthy and back home. Damn, it feels good to sleep in my own bed. We flew in late last night. I meant to call you all day today but it got away from me. I wanted to touch base and let you know that we're home."

"I thought you had another week on the island."

"Frankly, after everything that happened we just wanted to come home. Lisa and I discussed it and we've decided to have our second chance honeymoon later in the year. It felt like a different location might have better luck."

"Maybe something the opposite of tropical. You might want to try skiing."

"That's not a bad idea. So now that we're home, we want to get together with you and catch up. How about we schedule a dinner?"

"That sounds like a great idea. Can I bring a date?"

There was a short silence before Dan spoke again.

"Fuck yes, you can bring a date. I didn't realize you were even seeing anyone. That's why you came to the wedding alone."

"Things have changed since then."

For the better. I still couldn't believe that Emmy and I were a couple. Dammit, love hit me over the head without warning.

"So who's the lucky lady? Anyone we know?"

"Emmy," I said, holding my breath. We'd gone public with her friends but not mine. This was the first step. "We sort of hit it off on the island. Spent a lot of time together that weekend."

"Emmy," Dan breathed. "Wow, she's...fantastic. That's great."

His hesitation wasn't lost on me.

"You don't seem sure."

There was some coughing and then Dan cleared his throat. "Shit, Emmy is wonderful. Gorgeous, smart, funny. She's the whole package."

That was half a sentence.

"But," I prompted impatiently. "Spit it out, my friend."

"It's just she seems really career-focused, that's all. Very dedicated."

"I'm career-focused, too. So are you. So is Lisa."

We were beyond all of that. Emmy was in this relationship all the way.

"You're right. Don't fucking listen to me, man. I'm sleep deprived and don't know what I'm talking about. It sounds like you're happy. So let's schedule dinner, okay? We can't wait to see you. And Emmy."

"Let me check with her and see when she's free. I'll text you. And give my love to Lisa, okay? I'm glad she's on the mend."

"You and me both."

We both signed off and I set my phone on the bedside table. Just in case Emmy called. In the meantime, I had about ten thousand emails I needed to read. The work simply never ended. At least I had a woman that understood.

Emmy

We followed Shelby to her bedroom where she stopped at the foot of the bed and pointed to it accusingly.

"We can start with this. I wanted a white comforter but Brad said that it was impractical and it would get too dirty. We'd spend all our time washing it." She threw up her hands and made an impatient sound. "As if Brad was ever going to do a fucking load of laundry. I was the one that was going to wash it if it got dirty so if I was okay with it, why did he throw a fucking fit? Why, I ask you?"

I didn't have an answer but I sort of agreed with Brad. Keeping a white comforter clean sounded like a daily nightmare even in the absence of pets.

Swinging her attention from the comforter, Shelby shook her finger directly at me. "And don't tell me that white isn't practical. I know it's not practical. I just want it. Is that too much to ask? Is it?"

Her voice had gone up precipitously at the end and I immediately shook my head at her query. "No, it's not. If you want that, then you should have it."

But it was going to need washing pretty much every single week.

I didn't have time to dwell on that though as Shelby marched into the ensuite bathroom, Ashlyn and I on her heels.

"And look at this," she said, pointing to the standup shower. "I wanted a big bathtub with jets but instead I have this enormous shower cubicle. We could fit the entire Arborville police force in here and still have room to spare. I don't want to shower with friends, I want to soak in a gigantic tub with jets pointed at the sore spots on my back."

"Honey," Ashlyn said in a gentle tone. "Then why did you agree to the large shower? It's not like you to not get what you want."

That was an understatement.

"Because I thought I was compromising, and that's important in any relationship. A person can't have everything their own way."

The words popped out of my mouth before I could stop them. "That's the most depressing thing I've ever heard."

Ashlyn scowled and Shelby looked at me as if I had two heads.

I shrugged and leaned against the bathroom doorway. "What? Well, it is. Wouldn't it be great if we could have it all just the way we wanted it?"

"It's not realistic," Shelby snapped back at me. "This is why you're single."

"You're probably right."

I didn't want to argue with my friend, not when she was feeling like shit.

"Actually, Emmy has a–" Ashlyn began, but I cut her off.

"That's not important right now. What's important is Shelby getting all this anger and resentment off her chest. She needs to express that."

Shelby nodded, standing taller. "Damn skippy, I need to express it. Follow me. There's more. I swear from this day forward I'm not going to be so easy to get along with. I'm going to fight for what I really want. If I want white cabinets, then I'm fucking going to get white kitchen cabinets, and he can shove his cherry cabinets up his ass. I wonder if Kimberly likes cherry cabinets?"

I preferred a dark wood in the kitchen to cover fingerprints, maybe an espresso stain on the wood. Shelby really liked white furnishings and fixtures, but then she liked to clean. She said it cleared her mind of all the cobwebs. Tequila could do that, too.

Despite the fact that Shelby had said the word *cabinets* about fifty times in the last two minutes, this wasn't about cabinets at all. This was about Brad being a whiner and getting his own way. He didn't even live here full-time. He had his own condo a few miles away, although he spent four or five nights a week with Shelby.

It appeared that he'd been a busy boy on those other nights with *Kimberly*. How long had that been going on?

Shelby was a trained relationship psychologist and she'd picked the wrong man. What chance did a regular person have? What chance did I have?

Slim to none, that's what. I was doomed.

CHAPTER TWENTY-THREE

Owen

FRIDAY NIGHT, EMMY and I were meeting Dan and Lisa for dinner at the barbecue place downtown. I hadn't seen much of her during the week. Between her work commitments and Shelby's wrecked love life, she was booked up.

We had managed a quick lunch on Tuesday – a shared bag of takeout eaten on Emmy's desk – and a dinner on Wednesday night with her friends. Shelby had dominated that evening, discussing her breakup, her ex, and weighing her options going forward. I encouraged her to do things she would have never done with Brad, and Emmy had agreed enthusiastically. Ashlyn had suggested that Shelby call another one of their friends named Gibson, who was a contractor, and get an estimate for making renovations to her home. From what Shelby had said, she'd made several compromises for Brad when she'd purchased the house. Now she could customize it any way she'd like.

That wasn't much alone time and even though we were having dinner with friends I was hoping that later Emmy and I could spend some quality time together.

No, I don't mean sex.

Okay, I kind of mean sex.

Except that it would be fine if we didn't have sex. I'm not a maniac or anything. I can go without if I need to and trying to persuade an exhausted woman to fuck me didn't sound romantic or fun. I still owed her a back rub, after all.

I just wanted to have some time with Emmy that was just us. Cuddling, talking, whatever. I was in love with her so it only made sense. It's just that this week I hadn't felt close to her at all. She hadn't wanted to talk except about work or Shelby. Even when I hugged or kissed her, she hadn't melted into my arms. She'd been…distant. I didn't want to push, though. She, Shelby, and Ashlyn were as close as sisters and if one was hurting that meant they all were.

I simply wanted to let her know that I was here for her. With Shelby demanding every bit of Emmy's time and attention I didn't want to be the guy that was demanding shit, too.

Dan and Lisa arrived at the restaurant before us so they already had a table and were waving at us when we walked in. Emmy's face lit up with a smile when she saw how healthy that Lisa looked.

"She bounced back fast," Emmy said. "She's a marvel of modern medicine."

Placing my arm around her waist, I pulled her close to my side. She always smelled amazing and tonight was no exception – the delicate scent of vanilla with a hint of floral that made my heart beat faster. "She's a newlywed and in love."

"The magic of love?"

The way Emmy said it didn't sound positive.

"Yes, but then you know my opinion about that."

I'd been pretty damn vocal back in the Caribbean. Emmy

wasn't completely on board but I'd hoped that recent events might have softened her stance.

Like falling in love.

She hadn't said it out loud but I swear I could see it in her eyes when we made love. It was only then that she seemed to lower that emotional fortress she'd built and simply let herself be.

Dinner with Dan and Lisa was fun and we all laughed at their story about traveling back to Illinois. They'd had a hell of a time, first a delay due to a mechanical malfunction and then being rerouted to Dallas because of weather. They'd been happy and grateful to arrive home in one piece.

"The night is young," I said after we took care of the check and headed out into the cool night air. Not cold anymore, but still chilly. "There's a karaoke bar just around the corner. Who's game?"

Dan's face instantly lit up as I knew it would. Lisa rolled her eyes at her husband but was smiling, so she was in as well. Emmy? She was wearing a dubious expression and describing it that way was being kind.

She actually looked scared as hell.

"You don't like karaoke? It really is fun." Lisa elbowed me in the ribs. "This guy is crazy for it."

This obviously came as a surprise to Emmy since the topic had never come up before.

"It's not that I don't like it." Emmy sighed and pulled the lapels of her jacket closer around her neck. "It's just...okay, here it is...I'm a terrible singer."

Dan grimaced. "Like a little off-key kind of bad or so bad

that people mistake you for a dying cat kind of bad?"

This time Lisa elbowed her new husband. "Honey, that was very rude."

Emmy shook her head. "No, it's fine. Sadly, it's more like the latter. I can't carry a tune in a bucket, so to speak. I've always wished I could sing but I just can't. I do sing in the car but I'm alone. That's my strict policy. I don't inflict my voice on innocent human beings."

The last thing I wanted was to make Emmy uncomfortable. Karaoke wasn't that important.

"We don't have–"

"We can go," she said quickly. "As long as you're okay with me not singing. I'll just enjoy everyone else."

"It's fine," I assured her. "Even if you could sing like Adele, we wouldn't force you."

"If I could sing like Adele, wild horses couldn't keep me off the stage," Emmy declared. "So what are we waiting for? Let's go."

★ ★ ★

Emmy

TRUE TO HIS word, Owen didn't try to get me to go onstage to sing, thank goodness. I still remember in second grade being placed in the back row and told to just mouth the words when the class was supposed to get up in front of the school and sing "Santa Claus is Coming to Town". My mom had bought me a brand-new outfit in Christmas red for that assembly and I thought I was really stylin'. I never did tell her that I wasn't actually singing. I didn't want her to be disappointed.

Luckily, the entire atmosphere of the club was laid back and relaxed. More upscale than the usual college watering hole, the entire place was done up in dark oak – floor, tables, and chairs. The small stage was on the far wall with one lone spotlight illuminating the entertainers.

The clientele was well-behaved and supportive no matter how bad the singer, which I thought was nice of them. One young woman basically destroyed "Somewhere Over the Rainbow" but no one booed, instead politely clapping when she was done. Perhaps they were applauding the fact that she wasn't singing anymore. I sipped at my glass of wine as Lisa and Dan went up on stage and sang an amazing rendition of "Don't Go Breaking My Heart". They were truly talented, and they made the most adorable couple ever. They were meant for each other.

I couldn't stop, however, an image of Shelby and Brad drifting through my brain. They'd been happy once too, and now look at them. Or at least, look at Shelby. She was a mess. She was a freakin' professional in relationships and she'd still been blindsided.

Maybe being lucky in love was completely random. It didn't matter who or what you were, you weren't in charge. It was the arbitrary nature of the universe that decided whether you got true love or got dumped. A person might do better playing roulette in Vegas.

Do ya' feel lucky, punk?

Did I?

Clearing his throat, Owen dropped a quick kiss on my lips before standing. Even just that brief touch sent a quick zip of electricity up my spine. "It's my turn so I guess I better do this. If I'm bad, I give you all permission to pretend you don't know me."

I would never do that.

He bounded up the three steps to the stage and stood in front of the microphone. All alone up there. It took balls, I'd give him that.

"I wouldn't stand up there and sing for all the money in the world," I vowed. "As in never ever."

"I bet you're not as bad as you think," Lisa said excitedly, grabbing my hand. "But he's really good."

"I am as bad as I think."

Owen, on the other hand, was better than I'd expected. Really, really good. He sang the rock ballad "Amanda" from the seventies band Boston. His gaze never left mine as he sang and my heart squeezed painfully in my chest the whole song. It was clear he was singing those loving lyrics to me. *Me.* I'd never had a man do anything more romantic in my entire efficient and practical life.

Do ya' feel lucky, punk?

Good question.

Don't fall for the magic. It lies.

Was I being played for a fool?

Flowers, candy, and love songs. It's the oldest game in town.

I'd always been good at games.

That squeezing in my chest had given way to a feeling of desperate panic. My pulse racing and my breathing shallow, I greeted Owen as enthusiastically as I could, but deep inside I was looking at him with suspicion. When was he going to pull the rug from under me?

Do ya' feel lucky, punk?

No, I wasn't going to let doubt creep in. He'd just sung a love song to me.

Fuck you.

No, fuck you.

It was like having an optimist and pessimist on my shoulders, each one shouting in my ear trying to get me to believe that their truth was the only truth. I wanted to brush them away and tell them to leave me the hell alone.

"I need some air," I announced loudly as Owen ordered us another round. I jumped up from my chair, anxious to get some space around me. I needed to run away from my thoughts, but I had a feeling they'd only follow me. "And the ladies room. Wherever it is."

"I'll go with you," Lisa said, gathering up her purse. "I can direct you. It's near the front doors."

I couldn't be rude and tell her that I didn't want company so I instead smiled and thanked her. Turning to go, I was stopped by Owen's fingers gently wrapping around my wrist.

"How about a kiss before you go?"

"Of course," I replied, obediently bending down to brush my lips against his. They were warm and firm, tasting of the craft beer he'd been drinking. "I'll be right back."

I followed Lisa to the ladies room, shutting myself into a stall so I could have a moment. Just a minute to breathe. In the main room it had felt like the walls were closing in on me. So many questions, so many doubts. I knew how I felt about Owen and I wanted to believe that he felt the same.

Taking another cleansing breath, I stepped out of the stall and stood next to Lisa who was freshening up her lipstick. With hands that trembled visibly, I did the same.

"Owen looks really happy," Lisa said, capping her lipstick and dropping into her bag. "He's a great guy and you two make a terrific couple. If I'd known you two would hit it off like this, I would have introduced you to him months ago."

"He's a great guy," I agreed, trying to control my shaking fingers. This wasn't what I'd wanted when I'd walked away from the table. I'd wanted space and Lisa telling me how wonderful Owen was… That was pressure.

"He's one of a kind," Lisa went on, fluffing her long hair. "Kind, smart, and successful. He's been looking for the right woman for a long time. I know that he's ready to settle down. He's tired of the dating games."

Jeebus on a cracker, what did she want me to say? Was I supposed to gush and tell her how much I loved him? I liked Lisa a whole lot but I wasn't the gushing or confessing type with people I wasn't close to. Shelby, Ashlyn, or Mia might get me to spill my guts but it wasn't happening in this public bathroom.

"I think we all are when we get over thirty."

A nice, neutral answer.

Lisa pushed open the door and the sounds of the nightclub rushed in to the bathroom, echoing off the walls. It was time to go back to the table. I couldn't think of any reason not to other than I wasn't ready. Could I fake a heart attack? The way it was pounding I think I could do it.

We stepped out into the hallway that led to the main room. Lisa slung her purse over her shoulder and gave me a wide smile.

"I just want to say how happy Dan and I are that you and Owen have found each other."

I was *found.* Had I been lost? Had Owen been lost? Was this more of the magic of love stuff? You could walk around lost but get yourself some love and you're found. Praise Cupid.

"I like Owen a lot," I heard myself saying. "But right now I'd describe our relationship as casual. You know what I mean."

If Lisa did, she didn't get a chance to say so as we walked through the small foyer of the club. The world turned upside down when my eyes met Owen's standing in that doorway to the outside, phone in hand. He must have exited to take a call because a person couldn't hear a thing inside.

He didn't look happy.

Fuck, this wasn't good. Had he heard what I'd said or was he just pissed off because of the conversation he'd just ended?

I had a feeling I was going to find out.

Shit and double shit. I could explain. I didn't mean what he thinks I said. Right?

CHAPTER TWENTY-FOUR

Owen

CASUAL. EMMY HAD called our relationship *casual.* It was like a knife in my heart.

I'd walked back into the club after taking a phone call only to hear the woman I adored and loved calling what we had casual. As in non-important. No big deal. Practically a friendship. It fucking hurt.

Hoping I'd heard wrong, I didn't say anything to her about it for the rest of the evening. By ten we were all ready to go home, so we bid Dan and Lisa goodbye and I bundled Emmy into the car. The drive back to her place was quiet and I could feel the tension build with every passing traffic light. When we reached her place, I still didn't know exactly what I was going to say but I wasn't one to sweep issues under the rug. Maybe it was the psychologist in me but I was all about airing things out. Talk and resolve.

"Do you want a beer or a glass of wine?" she asked me as we shed our coats. She'd barely looked at me in the last hour and a half. "You can turn on the television of you like."

"I don't really want to watch tv," I replied, watching her flit around the room turning on lamps and plumping throw pillows.

She was nervous and so was I. This was our first big discussion as a couple. "I think we should talk, Emmy."

"That's never a good statement," she said, her voice shaky. "What do you want to talk about?"

"What you said to Lisa tonight," I replied, settling onto the couch. If I had a relaxed demeanor, I hoped that she would relax as well. "I'll admit that it upset me, Emmy."

I kept my tone even, not wanting to heighten the tension any more than it already was. I wanted to discuss this like two adults. I wasn't looking to start an argument.

This time Emmy did sit on the couch but just out of arm's reach. "I didn't mean to upset you."

She sounded like a prim schoolmarm. Not a good sign.

"Can you tell me in what context you said we were only casual? Because I'd hoped we had moved beyond all of this."

The key word being *hoped*.

Her fingers tightly laced together, Emmy answered. "Lisa was saying that she thought we made a nice couple and that she and Dan were so glad that you and I had found each other. Honestly, it felt like she wanted me to speak about our relationship and I'm not comfortable revealing intimate details to just anyone. My close friends are one thing but Lisa and I don't have that sort of friendship. So I guess I just wanted to say something to get her to back off a little bit."

That wasn't so bad. Emmy definitely was not the type of female that divulged intimate secrets to someone in the ladies' room of a nightclub. It was one of the reasons that I'd fallen for her. She had an innate class that I admired.

"And of course," Emmy went on. "We haven't been dating

all that long. I mean…less than a month so it didn't seem out of line to say that we were at a casual stage."

It wasn't at all out line but it was far from how I felt about Emmy.

"I can understand why you said what you said. Lisa had had a few drinks so she may not have realized how she was coming across."

Emmy nodded in agreement. "I'm not saying a word against Lisa. She's a real sweetheart. I just think we might have a different attitude about sharing personal information, that's all. Are we okay? I truly didn't mean to upset you."

"It's fine," I assured her because it was. All of my doomsday thoughts during the drive here had turned out to be false. Scooting across the couch cushions, I lifted her onto my lap, kissing her deeply, our tongues coming out to play. "If they only knew just how far from casual we really are. You make me crazy, Em."

She pressed a series of kisses on my jawline while her fingers tangled in my hair. My cock jumped behind my fly, instantly ready for action. As always with this woman.

"You make me crazy, too," she giggled, plucking at a button on my shirt.

The feel of Emmy in my arms was overwhelmingly pleasurable. She was the one that I'd been waiting for all of this time.

"I'm so glad you did Dan and Lisa's wedding, and I'm so glad that we met." I captured her lips again, pulling her as close to me as possible. "Emmy, I love you."

Honestly, I hadn't been planning to say it but it had come tumbling out of my mouth and now that I'd said it out loud, I didn't regret it. It was the way that I felt, dammit. I loved Emmy. It was the truth and I wasn't going to take it back.

I don't know what I thought would happen after I'd said it. Maybe that she'd kiss me and tell me she loved me, too. Then she'd drag me back into her bedroom and we'd shag until dawn.

Neither of those things happened.

Emmy pulled back and stared at me, her eyes wide in…fright? Surprise? It sure as shit wasn't happiness because if anything she appeared to be distressed by my admission.

This had been going well until I opened my big damn mouth. Fuck. My heart had stopped beating in my chest and I held my breath waiting for her reply.

No going back. I could only plow forward. The first question on my lips was the most difficult.

Did she love me, too?

I didn't ask it. Because I was too busy holding my breath.

"Are you okay?"

It was the second question that came to my mind because Emmy looked like she wanted to pass out, vomit, or cry. Not necessarily in that order.

She nodded but her gaze had shifted away from me. Well…fuck. I knew where this was going.

"I'm fine. I just…wow…I wasn't prepared for that."

Clearly. Now I felt like a fucking idiot.

But I would have sworn that she felt the same. Where had I gone wrong?

"I'm not trying to pressure you." I really wasn't. "I kind of thought you might feel the same."

I'd seen it in her eyes, dammit. I wasn't some teenage boy

who didn't have a clue. I was a grown ass man that had been around people in love pretty much my entire career.

"I think maybe you do love me, Emmy. Does that sound terrible? I'm not trying to be a jerk, it's just that I've seen love a lot in my life and I think we've got it right here. What we have is special."

"It is," she agreed readily. "It definitely is."

Okay, that wasn't so bad.

I was nervous so I started to ramble a bit.

"We're adults, honey, and we don't need months and months to figure out how we feel about each other. When you find the one, you just know."

"You're right."

She was agreeing with her mouth but her body language wasn't following suit. What was going on here?

"Emmy," I said gently, rubbing her back with my palm and trying to put her at ease. She was holding herself so stiffly. "Am I pushing you too hard? Just tell me to back off."

Lifting her gaze to mine, she opened her mouth to speak but then closed it again. Her eyes were bright with unshed tears and I felt about two inches tall. I'd fucked up and now I felt terrible. I could clearly see the battle she was fighting inside. Whatever she wanted to say, she was barely holding it in.

"You need to express yourself, honey. Say whatever it is that you want to say. I can take it."

"Shelby," she croaked, a few of those tears spilling over and sliding down her creamy cheeks. I reached up to brush them away but she shook her head, sitting up and moving to another chair. Whatever she wanted to say she needed some space to do it.

"What about Shelby, honey? I know you're worried about your friend but she's going to be fine. She's a strong woman. It may take some time but she's going to get through this."

Dashing away her tears with the back of her hand, Emmy took a deep breath and sat up straight. "It's just that if Shelby can be heartbroken, what chance do the rest of us mere mortals have? I mean…is it all just random? Is it a game of chance? There doesn't appear to be any rhyme or reason to who gets true love and who doesn't."

"Shelby just made a bad choice. I think when she's had some time she'll look back and tell you there were warning signs."

Emmy seemed to jump on that statement, leaning forward in eagerness. "When? When were these so-called warning signs? And if she was a professional, why didn't she see them? Fuck, Owen, she wrote a book about dating and relationships and hers crashed and burned spectacularly."

"I don't know when the signs would have shown themselves," I explained slowly, watching Emmy's expression closely while my heart sank to my stomach. We were back to where we started. We hadn't made any progress at all. "And as for why she didn't see them, she was too close. It's much easier to step back and be unbiased when it isn't about you."

"Exactly," Emmy said immediately. "You can't be unbiased in your own relationship. You can only hope and pray that you haven't fucked up. That doesn't seem like a great way to run your life."

It was frustration that made the next words pop out of my mouth.

"You mean it's not efficient?"

She sat up straight in the chair and glared. "If you want to know the truth, then yes. It's not very efficient or practical. It sucks, actually. A person can do everything right and still get punched in the heart. What kind of world is that?"

"I'm sure you've seen–"

"You have no idea what I've seen," she interrupted, her lips pressed together in a thin line. "I've comforted both brides and grooms when they've been left high and dry. You know what they all ask? What did I do wrong? I never know what to tell them. I can only say that I don't think they did anything wrong. So what did Shelby do wrong, Owen? What did she do to deserve this? What did they all do to deserve this? I need to know."

"Shelby didn't do anything and neither did those brides and grooms. But that can't be all you've seen. I know that you've had happy, loving couples that are still married. You told me that you've done fifty-year wedding anniversaries and baby showers. Aren't those people happy?"

"That's what I'm trying to ask." Emmy slapped the arm of the chair, her expression stormy. "Why do they have the luck and not Shelby? She's a good person. Karma doesn't need to be worrying about her. Why was she bitchsmacked by love? It doesn't make sense."

"I don't know. It's about finding the right person. It's about someone that meshes with your–"

"If you and Shelby don't know then how can anyone know?" she said irritably. "You've studied relationships your entire adult life and you don't have any more answers than I do."

"Now wait a minute," I protested, holding up my hands. "You're taking what I'm saying and twisting it. There are ways to predict how well a couple is going to do but the rest is up to them. There's always that unknowable spark between two people that can't be defined but when it's there, you know."

Her shoulders slumped and she fell back against the chair cushion. "The magic of love."

"For want of a better term? Yes, there's a bit of sorcery to love, Emmy. It can't be all defined and pinned down. It's part science and part magic. But don't you see, that's what makes it so special and exciting."

From the look on her face I might as well have been speaking Swahili. She didn't get it and that was sad.

"You see it in your job every day," I pressed. "But you choose to concentrate on the ones that don't make it instead of the ones that do."

"And you concentrate on the opposite," she argued. "Is one way any better than the other?"

I opened my mouth to answer and then snapped it shut but she'd already noticed.

"You were going to say that your way is better. My way is wrong."

"It's just more negative," I finally answered, trying desperately to find the right words. "It's not going to make you happy in the end to always focus on what could go wrong. Every day bad things can happen but we don't dwell on them. I could get in a car accident or choke on a hamburger but I don't live my life avoiding cars and cheeseburgers."

There was a long silence and then Emmy sighed and rubbed

her hand over her temple.

"Maybe I don't make any sense, but after seeing what Shelby's going through, it's reminded me that no one knows shit about love. Especially me. And if that's true, wouldn't it be prudent for me to be cautious?"

Yes. No. Fuck.

"I just know that I love you, Emmy, and I think that you love me, too." I didn't know what else to say. "Love doesn't always make sense. It's not always logical."

"That's what is so scary."

"I'm not trying to scare you."

"I know, and I'm sorry that I am. But I can't help it."

We'd gone around and around and were back where we started.

"Is what you told Lisa what you really want, Emmy? Do you want me to back off and give you space?"

She didn't answer right away, instead staring down at her hands as if they held the secrets to the universe. When she finally did look up, I knew her answer without her even having to say it.

"I just need to slow down."

There it was. What I'd been dreading.

"I thought we'd moved on from this. I thought we were doing fine."

My heart squeezed in my chest making it hard to breathe. Fear had taken up residence in my gut, churning up the acid until I could taste it at the back of my throat.

"We were, we are," she assured me, her gaze intense. "I just need..."

Her voice trailed away as if she didn't want to finish her

thoughts. Because they would hurt me.

"Space. Without me in it."

I'd tried to make a joke but it wasn't all that funny. She was ripping my heart out of my chest with her bare hands.

"It's all just happening so fast."

At this point I couldn't help but agree.

"Maybe you're right. Maybe we've moved too fast. I thought you were opening up to the idea of love, Emmy, but I can see that I was wrong."

Sure, I sounded bitter because I damn well was fucking bitter. I'd let myself fall for Emmy but clearly, she'd only been half in when I'd been all the way.

"Please don't be angry with me."

Her voice was soft and I could hear the hurt in her tone. I wanted to reach out and comfort her but I was too wounded at the moment to be so magnanimous. She'd taken a hammer and smashed me right in the heart. That wasn't going to put a guy in a great mood.

"I'm not angry with you, Emmy. I'm mad at myself." I stood, not wanting to prolong this agony any longer. She wasn't going to suddenly change her mind and tell me it was all a rotten joke. "I think I should go."

I shrugged into my coat as she hovered nearby, probably not knowing what to say any more than I did. Fuck. Everything had been going so well and then this situation with Shelby had thrown it all into disarray.

When my hand went to the doorknob, she finally spoke. "What happens now?"

Since I hadn't predicted any of this, I had no fucking idea.

"I don't know. You're the one that wants space and time. I guess that's up to you."

Yep, I sounded like an asshole. I'd be sorry about it later but right now it was the only thing that made me feel better. Making her hurt just a fraction of what I did.

"You are angry at me."

"Frustration and anger are two different emotions, Emmy. Shit, I don't want to argue with you."

"I don't want to argue with you, either." A tear carved a path down her cheek. "I can't be someone that I'm not, Owen."

"I can't either," I shot back, the pain in my abdomen and heart almost unbearable. That's what made me lash out. "Maybe this isn't going to work."

I heard her indrawn breath. "Are you ending things?"

"I don't know what to do," I confessed, tears burning behind my eyes. "I'm totally blindsided about all of this. A few hours ago, I thought we were happy and falling in love. Now I find out that we're going too fast and you need space. I think I should give it to you. Take all of the time you need."

"That's sounds final."

I was officially done with this conversation. I wanted out of here before I said even more that I would regret later.

"It's whatever you want it to be. If you don't want me, then I wish you all the best in finding someone to love and have a life with. But I will say this, Emmy, it's not fair to jerk me around and then act like you have no idea what I'm talking about. You said you were in and now I find out you're not. You want to talk about being fair? Well, that's not it."

Now I'd made her cry for real. Three cheers for me being a

douche. But I couldn't seem to shut up.

"I was in. I do care."

"But now you don't?"

"I just…" She slapped her hand over her mouth and shook her head. "I don't know what to say."

"That makes two of us. If you ever figure it out, give me a call. But I have a feeling I shouldn't bother waiting by the phone."

And because I'm a jerk who liked getting the last word in an argument, I pushed open the door and lumbered down the front steps. I desperately wanted to turn around but I wouldn't let myself. No, no, no. I wouldn't let her know how deeply she'd wounded me. I was shocked that I wasn't covered in blood, it was so real and painful. Emmy had pulled the rug from under me and then shoved in the knife.

I was off to lick my wounds. After that? I had no fucking idea.

CHAPTER TWENTY-FIVE

Emmy

After Owen stomped out, I curled up on the couch and cried myself to sleep, feeling more miserable than I could ever remember. I'd messed it all up, and I didn't know what to do to fix it. What he'd said was true, we were happy. I simply couldn't trust that it would continue.

When I woke, my neck and back hurt because I'd folded myself into an origami swan while I slept. It did nothing to better my mood, nor did a scalding cup of coffee that burned my esophagus on the way down. Still dressed in my clothes from last night, I sipped at the bitter liquid, replaying the scene between us.

Getting more pissed off with each passing second.

It had all been a trap. Not that he'd set it on purpose but the result was the same. He'd placed me neatly in a corner and I was supposed to respond just the way he'd wanted me to.

Fuck him. Just who did he think he was?

My life had been fine and dandy before Owen Campbell and it was going to be just as good after. Hell, it was going to be even better. I didn't need a man, and honestly, I wasn't sure I really wanted one.

First, they were a lot of work. Hygiene-wise. When I'm not dating anyone I can let my legs go unshaved for a few days, especially in the cold weather when I'm always wearing pants. Heck, I might even skip an extra day of not washing my hair and just pull it up into a ponytail.

When you're dating, you can't do that. You have to have freshly shaved legs, pits, and bikini line at all times. You know…just in case.

Second, you now have to think about another person's wants. Let's say I want Chinese takeout but Owen wants Italian. I can't just say fuck you and get Chinese. That would make me a bitch and a bad girlfriend. I have to think about who chose last time and who had the worse day and all of that crap. Basically, who needs this the most?

Or maybe I like eating in bed and watching television but he thinks that the bed is only for sleeping and sex and hates crumbs in the sheets. Do I have to stop eating in bed?

I still didn't know the answer to that one. It was probably yes but I couldn't be sure.

Third, when you're a couple you're supposed to act like a couple. You get invited as a couple and you go as a couple. If he's having a great time at a party and I think it stinks, I might have to stay because I'm part of a couple now. Or vice versa.

It's a bunch of work and I don't know why women everywhere weren't completely exhausted.

Slamming my empty cup into the sink, I stomped into the foyer where I'd left my purse and keys. I needed to see Shelby right away.

Slinging my purse over my shoulder, I caught sight of my

reflection in the mirror on the wall.

Hair standing almost straight up. Makeup smeared. I looked like a raccoon with mascara under my eyes. Clothes were wrinkled as if I'd slept in them. Which I had.

New plan. A shower and then I'd go see Shelby.

It was time for the new and improved Emmy, and I was ready to have some fun.

★ ★ ★

Owen

I TOSSED THE folder down onto my desk and growled in frustration. Nothing was right today and everyone had banded together to piss me off.

Carly, who headed up my team of assistants, picked the folder up and waved it in front of my face like a red flag in front of a charging bull.

"What's wrong with it now? You've been like a bear with a sore paw all day. No one wants to come near you. My team practically begged me on their knees not to talk to you. Is this some new management strategy or are you just being an asshole?"

"Maybe I'm just an asshole," I snarled, reaching for a bottle of water and chugging half of it down in one gulp. "Maybe if your team can't take the heat then they should find other jobs."

Dumping the folder and two binders on my desk, Carly whirled on her heel and marched over to my office door to slam it shut before marching back and pointing a finger directly at my chest.

"Sit down."

"I don't–"

"I don't give a shit what you want," she interrupted, her face now red. "Sit the fuck down and then tell me what the hell's your problem."

"I don't–"

"Sit down."

This time her voice had dropped even lower almost sounding demon-like. Carly didn't often lose her temper but I had a feeling I was tiptoeing on the line with her.

So I sat the fuck down in my oversized leather chair and reminded myself why I had it. I was the goddamn boss and if I wanted to be a jerk then I could be. She wasn't going to tell me how to act.

"Carly–"

"I'm talking. You don't get to talk yet. I'll let you know when it's your turn."

"I'm not going to take this–"

"Yes, you are." She shook a finger at me. "You're going to sit there and listen. I don't what crawled up your ass and died last night or this morning but everyone in this office has had it with your attitude today. You're scaring your own employees and they don't have to put up with this crap. You don't get to be a douchebag just because you own the joint."

"Actually, I think I do."

I'd managed to get a word in but Carly was less than pleased.

"Did I say you could talk? No, I did not. So hush your mouth. Your turn will come." She took a deep breath and dropped down into one of my guest chairs. "Now tell me what your problem is or I swear I will quit and you don't even know where we keep the pens in this place."

"I can have pens delivered."

I didn't sound all that sure, though.

Carly was more than willing to call my bluff. She pulled her cell phone out of her pocket and thumbed the screen. "Fine, I'll call Jake and tell him I'm now a stay at home mom. He's going to be thrilled."

Jake would be, too.

"Don't you dare call Jake," I finally said with a heavy sigh. "I don't want you to quit."

Tucking the phone back in her pocket, Carly smiled triumphantly. "I think you've made a wise choice. Now spill it. Why are you acting like Satan today? And be specific."

Sitting back in the chair, I thought about all that had passed between Emmy and I last night. What we'd said and didn't say. What still needed to be said. And all the things I could have done a hell of a lot better.

"I think Emmy and I might have broken up last night."

"You're not sure?"

"I'm not. We definitely argued and I walked out."

Carly tapped her chin with a pen. "Send flowers, apologize for whatever you did, and then it will all be okay."

Now wait a minute…

"It isn't all my fault," I argued. "She started it. She's the one that said she wanted to slow down."

Her phone chimed in her pocket and she pulled it out, making a face. "I have to pick up Sara from dance practice. Listen, how about you and I go to dinner? Just the two of us. I'll get

Jake to watch the kids and then you and I can talk about this. You can tell me the whole story and I'll give you whatever wisdom I may have. If you did break up, I don't want you sitting at home brooding about it. You need to get out and be around people."

It was the last thing I wanted, which made me decide that it was probably what I needed.

"Sounds like a plan. I'll pick you up about seven."

"Deal." She leaned forward and that finger was back, shaking under my nose. "Now go home. Go to the gym. Go for a run. Do something, but don't stay here. You're going to piss off the employees and you don't want them to quit en masse, do you?"

I didn't, although my behavior said something far different.

"I could go to the gym. A workout might make me feel better."

Carly stood and picked up her things. "If you and Emmy did break up, I am sorry. She sounded like she might have been the one."

I'd thought so, too.

★ ★ ★

"WE NEED A girls' night out."

That's what I said to Shelby when she let me into her home an hour later when I looked much more human and less like an extra from "The Walking Dead".

"Hello to you too, Emmy."

Shelby looked better as well. She'd taken a shower recently

and was wearing clean clothes without stains. That was real progress.

Tossing my purse onto a chair, I headed straight for her kitchen. "Do you have coffee made, by any chance?"

"There's half a pot. Help yourself."

I did and enjoyed that first sip of the dark brew. Shelby knew how to make a pot of coffee.

"We need a girls' night out," I repeated, wrapping my hands around the hot mug and leaning a hip against the kitchen counter. The sink was clear of dishes which was a good sign. Shelby had been cleaning. "Are you in?"

Scowling, Shelby topped off her own coffee cup. "Tell me why we need this, because I'd made plans for the foreseeable future to never leave my house unless I was forced to."

I took another sip before answering.

"I think Owen and I broke up last night."

She blinked once...twice...then a third time.

"Okay then. Did you call Ashlyn?"

"Not yet. Do you think she'd be our designated driver?"

I'd thought I might have to beg and plead to get Shelby to go. This was unexpected.

"You're fine with this? When I say a girls' night out, I mean tonight. Not in a few weeks."

Shelby nodded over the edge of her mug. "I know what you mean."

"And you want to go?"

"No, but you do, and right now I need to think about someone other than myself. I'm so tired of feeling sorry for myself. I'm seriously sick of...me."

"We'll have fun."

"So what happened with Owen?"

I shrugged as if I didn't care. Because I didn't. "The usual. He wanted more than I was ready to give. Blah, blah, blah. I'm already over it."

"That was fast."

"I'm a quick healer."

"Normally I'd ask if you want to talk about it but frankly, I'm not in the mood."

"That makes two of us. Talking doesn't help. Tequila does."

"I couldn't agree more. Should we call Ashlyn?"

"Why don't we just go to her shop and kidnap her? Then she can't say no."

I didn't know exactly what we were going to do but I wanted it to be so much fun that I wouldn't remember any of it the next day. I didn't need Dr. Owen Campbell.

Let the games begin.

CHAPTER TWENTY-SIX

Owen

CARLY AND I ended up at a bistro in the downtown area. We both ordered our food and let the waitress walk back to the kitchen before digging into the real reason we were there.

"Emmy pulled the rug out from under me," I explained, sipping on an ice-cold glass of beer. "I don't think she believes in love. It's two steps forward and three steps back with her."

"So you told her you loved her?" Carly asked. "And she didn't say it back?"

"Exactly. That's exactly what happened."

I could still see Emmy's face from last night, clear as day.

"But you must have thought that she was going to say it back," Carly pointed out. "Or else you wouldn't have said it, right?"

"That's true," I conceded with a grimace. "I thought she loved me but I guess I was wrong. You should have seen her expression when I told her. It was pure panic. I think she wanted to flee but we were standing in her house and it was cold outside. She wasn't wearing any shoes."

Carly simply regarded me for a long moment, not saying anything. She'd do this on occasion when she was thinking so I just let her have it. The waitress had dropped a basket of bread on the table so I grabbed a roll and smeared garlic butter on it.

"She was panicked? As in fear?"

"Yes."

"So you broke up with her?" Carly smacked the table, causing a few diners to swivel their heads toward the sound. "Owen, you are an idiot. Are you sure you have a doctorate in psychology because you're acting like you don't have two brain cells to rub together."

"Now wait a minute," I protested. "I didn't break up with her. Emmy wanted space so I gave it to her."

Carly waved her butter knife in a dramatic fashion. "And why did she want space?"

"She said she wanted us to slow down."

"But you didn't want to do that?"

Sighing, I took another drink of my beer. "I thought we were over that."

Shrugging, Carly raised her brows. "Well...you weren't."

"Thanks for the clarification."

"Clearly you needed it." Another sigh. This was getting repetitive. "Let me tell you a little story. It's one you've never heard. Are you listening to me?"

"Shit, I'm listening. Just tell it."

"Before I met Jake, I was dating this guy from grad school. Handsome, smart, funny. I thought he was the whole package. We had fun whenever we were together and I felt like he just really *got* me. You know what I mean?" She didn't pause for me to answer. "Anyway, I of course fell in love with him. I mean, who wouldn't? All my friends were jealous and I thought I'd found the one I was going to be with forever. I was planning for my mom and dad to meet him over the holidays. That's how sure I was."

This time she did pause, obviously waiting for a comment.

"But something happened."

Because something always happened in stories like this.

"Yes, something happened. I found out that he'd been seeing another girl the entire time we were dating. The entire time, Owen. When I confronted him about it, he acted like it was no big deal. As if we weren't even that serious and I was all angry for nothing. That just made me even angrier."

"How did you find out?"

Rubbing her temple, she shook her head. "That's not the right question. It doesn't matter how I found out. What mattered is that my heart was broken into about a million pieces and I didn't trust my judgment about men after that. I was sure every guy in the world was a big, fat liar and cheater and I wasn't going to be their victim ever again. So when I met Jake, he had an uphill battle, to say the least."

"But you two are together so obviously you didn't let what happened get in the way."

Carly tapped the surface of the table with her fingernail. "I made Jake's life hell. I was in, I was out, I was in, I was way out. I was confused and scared and generally a real pain in the ass. Do you know what he did?"

I couldn't wait to hear.

"He was patient with me. He waited me out. He didn't give up even when I pushed him away."

I'd had a sinking feeling that's what she was going to say.

Fuck. I'd screwed the pooch, hadn't I?

"So I'm slime? Is that what you're saying?"

"No, you're not slime. You are impatient and you think you know everything. News flash. You don't. You may be a relationship expert but you are not an expert on your own relationship. You're simply too close to it to be unbiased. I can stand to the side and see things more clearly. If Emmy is afraid of love, you storming out last night didn't cure that. If anything, it only confirmed that you weren't truly in it for the long haul."

"I fucked up," I admitted. It wasn't easy to say it out loud. "Now what do I do, oh wise one?"

Carly smiled and rubbed her hands together. "I'm so glad you asked. You have to go back to Emmy, apologize, and then hang in there. She's probably going to push you away again but you have to persevere even when it's tough."

"That sounds one-sided."

Carly was supposed to take my side of the argument. She was supposed to hear my story and then confirm that I was right and Emmy was in the wrong.

"It is," she nodded. "But listen to me carefully. You're asking her to put herself out there in the danger zone. You want her to risk her heart. You have to be willing to do it, too. There are no guarantees and she knows that. You have to know that, too. If she's worth it, go all the way for her."

"I have been risking my heart. I put myself out there."

Right?

"And at the first sign of a problem, you bailed. That's not much of a risk. You have to show her, Owen. Words aren't going to mean much here." Carly's gaze speared me, making me squirm with its intensity. "Is she worth it or not?"

Dammit, sometimes I hated my assistant. She wasn't supposed to be smarter than me.

"She's worth it."

"Then you know what you have to do."

★ ★ ★

ASHLYN HADN'T WANTED to take us out for the evening. She and her boyfriend Kyle had tried to talk us out of it, almost to their last breath, but Shelby and I were adamant. We wanted to go out and have some fun. With or without Ashlyn, we weren't fussy. We'd prefer if she went along but if she didn't want to go, that was fine, too.

When Kyle saw that we weren't going to be persuaded out of our harebrained idea – Ashlyn's words, not his – he immediately stepped into action. With more money than any one human being should have, he quickly hired a car service to drive us around in a black SUV with tinted windows.

Like we were rock stars.

The driver was a mountain of a man specifically hired by Kyle to protect us, which I thought was sweet but a tad over the top. We'd had many a girls' night out and hadn't needed a bodyguard.

They did manage to convince us to eat a good meal at Ashlyn's place before we set out. According to Kyle, full stomachs were the best way to slow down inebriation. I didn't really want to slow it down, though. I was welcoming it with open arms.

I let Shelby pick the bar and she chose the pub downtown that had darts, pool, and air hockey along with a decent music selection. The bartenders were always nice, the drinks weren't ten dollars apiece, and the bathrooms were clean.

The driver pulled up in front of the bar and parked before hopping out to open our door.

"Now let's pace ourselves," Ashlyn instructed as we tumbled out of the SUV. "You don't need to get drunk in the first half hour. We have all night."

We did have all night. Ashlyn's assistant Katie was going to open the store tomorrow, Shelby had cancelled her appointments, and my assistant Jana was handling any meetings tomorrow. We could sleep all day if we wanted to.

In a way it was funny for Ashlyn to be in charge like this. Normally it was Shelby bossing us around but for once she seemed content to simply go with the flow. I doubt it was going to last long, though. She was born to give orders.

"I'll be right out here," the driver said, holding up a cell phone. "You have my number, so if you need anything at all just text me. If some guys are hassling you or if you just want to go someplace else. Just let me know."

We all three had programmed his number in our phones. We were ready.

"So let's go," I said, tugging on Shelby's arm but she wasn't paying any attention to me or Ashlyn. Her gaze was focused farther down the sidewalk so I turned to see what was so interesting.

Owen.

It was *Owen* walking out of the bistro a few doors down and opening the car door for a very attractive woman. He held her hand as she stepped into the vehicle before going around to the driver's side and climbing in. He was actually smiling. He looked happy.

"Fuck, he didn't wait long, did he?" There was bitterness in my tone that I couldn't hide. "I guess if you own a dating site you can find a woman on short notice."

Her expression stricken, Shelby shook her head. "She wasn't someone he'd just met. He knew her well. You could tell by their comfortable body language."

Fantastic. That's just what I wanted to hear.

"You're not helping," Ashlyn whispered loudly to Shelby, giving her a sharp elbow in the ribs.

"So you're saying he might have been seeing her while he was seeing me?"

The bile rose in the back of my throat and I had to swallow hard to force it back down. Of all the things I'd thought about Owen, I'd never thought he would cheat.

Then why did you need time and space?

Shut up. I just wanted to move slow.

But you never thought he'd cheat?

No, I never did.

Then maybe you shouldn't have pushed for time. He might be with you right now.

"No, I'm not saying that," Shelby replied, completely unaware of the tumult inside of me. "What I'm saying is that they don't look like strangers. Maybe she's a coworker or a friend?"

"Maybe."

"I didn't get a real romantic vibe from them," Ashlyn declared, linking her arm with mine. "I don't think they're a couple."

I didn't answer right away, still staring at the parking space where Owen's car had been.

"It doesn't really matter whether it was romantic or not," I finally said. "Did you see his face? He's happy. He was having fun. He's not lying around listening to love ballads from the eighties. He's out having a good time less than twenty-four hours after our breakup."

"I hate to point this out but you're here to have fun tonight, too," Ashlyn said. "His being out may not mean anything."

I shook my head. She didn't get it. "He was out having actual fun and enjoying himself. I'm out hoping to have some fun and right now I can safely say that I'm not enjoying myself at all."

Shelby pointed to the door of the bar. "We're going to have fun tonight. I promise you. Now let's go. I'm buying the first round. Hell, I'm buying the first three rounds. And make them doubles."

Ashlyn closed her eyes and muttered under her breath. "Thank goodness Kyle has bail money."

Damn right we were going to have some fun. Bring on the limes and the tequila. The only man I wanted in my life at the moment was Jose Cuervo. He'd never let me down.

Yeehaw.

CHAPTER TWENTY-SEVEN

Emmy

DEATH…TAKE ME NOW.

No?

Shit, even death didn't want me.

My wish from yesterday was granted. There were definitely huge swaths of last night that I didn't remember. It was probably all for the best, if I were honest. I had vague memories of doing shots and dancing. On the table. Shelby at my side. We were like Butch and Sundance, Lucy and Ethel, Laurel and Hardy… You get the picture. She was my partner in crime and we'd had a ball.

Oh…and Ashlyn? She'd sort of watched in horror like Shelby and I were a car crash and she was a passing motorist. She may have taken a few photos for blackmail later as well.

Note to self: Check Ashlyn's phone.

I would do that just as soon as I managed to get up off the cold, unforgiving tile floor in Shelby's house. I'd slept curled up between the toilet and the bathtub. At some point in the night, someone had tucked a blanket around me. How thoughtful.

It couldn't have been Shelby because if I couldn't move then she sure as hell couldn't either. She was always saying she could hold her liquor the best of all four of us but that was bullshit with a capital B. She'd been head down in the toilet last night before we'd even left the bar.

That meant it was Ashlyn. It also meant that she must be the person that had brewed a pot of coffee. I could smell the lifesaving aroma even here in the bathroom and I desperately wanted a cup. Did I want it badly enough to move?

Yes. Yes, I did.

Easier said than done.

Every bone and muscle in my body ached as if someone had taken a sledgehammer to me last night. For all I know that had actually happened. It hurt so badly I almost changed my mind about getting up. I'd simply start my life over here in Shelby's spare bathroom. It was nice enough and it smelled like lemons.

But that aroma of coffee was tempting so I rolled over onto my hands and knees when I couldn't lever myself up from a sitting position. From there I was able to use the toilet bowl to push myself up without passing out or puking. I'll consider this a victory.

Wait. I'd just taken a look at myself in the mirror. This was no success story. I looked like a two-dollar crack ho that had been lying on a park bench for weeks. Hair standing on end, makeup smeared, clothes awry. I was also barefoot. When did I take off my shoes? And where were they?

Second note to self: Find shoes.

They'd been very expensive.

Like a ninety-year-old woman I creaked into the kitchen at a snail's pace, trying to smooth down my hair and failing miserably. Ashlyn stood at the counter popping bread into the toaster and I sent up a silent thank you that she hadn't decided to make bacon or pancakes. I couldn't have handled that.

"I heard you moving around so I thought I'd make some toast. It will help settle your stomach."

I almost asked why she thought I was nauseous and then an image of us doing shots floated through my head and I knew the answer.

"Shelby?" I asked, my voice a mere croak. I shuffled toward the coffeemaker, determined to get some of the magical brew.

"She's alive but asleep in bed. I've been checking on both of you throughout the night to make sure you hadn't choked on your own vomit."

Now that's a friend. Not only had she held my hair back when I had booted up Kyle's dinner, she'd made sure I was alive to do it again.

"Thank you." I reached for a cup out of the cabinets and filled it with coffee. The first sip tasted like ambrosia. "Oh, that is so good."

Ashlyn snorted and slapped a saucer down on the counter top. Loudly. "I want you to eat some of this toast."

If I didn't, she'd just bitch at me until I did and my head couldn't take that.

"I will."

The bread popped out of the toaster and it scared the ever-loving shit out of me. I simply wasn't prepared at this juncture of the morning and my hangover to deal with surprises. I almost spilled my coffee and Ashlyn had to grab my arm to keep me upright.

"Are you okay?"

"I've been better."

The dry toast was placed on the saucer.

"Eat this."

Wrinkling my nose, I took an experimental nibble. The world didn't end.

"For someone not in pain, you seem to be in a lousy mood. Care to share?"

For the first time that morning, Ashlyn finally looked up from her toaster and coffee.

"I'm a little miffed, actually."

"Because you didn't get drunk, too?"

Rolling her eyes, Ashlyn groaned. "No, because two of my best friends in the whole world are letting men bring them down. You and Shelby are the strongest people I know and here you are crawling this morning because you had too much tequila. It's not right."

Carefully I sat down at the kitchen island, making sure not to spill my coffee.

"Technically, I am the only one crawling. Shelby is still horizontal."

"You know what I mean."

Yes, I did. Sighing, I nodded. "Okay, it wasn't the smartest thing we've ever done but we're upset and hurt. I didn't intend to get that drunk but–"

I broke off, not wanting to put it all into words. That made it real.

"But? But when you saw Owen with another woman…"

"It hurt," I admitted, remembering how happy Owen had looked when I'd been miserable. "More than I thought it would."

"It's your own fault."

"Thank you, Ash, for the support."

Ashlyn's brows rose. "I think I gave you plenty of support last night and this morning. What you need is some truth to go with it. Normally that's what you and Shelby do but since neither of you is in a position to give it, and you won't let me tell Mia what's going on, then it falls to me. So get ready for some wisdom. Are you ready?"

I held up my coffee cup. "Can I get a refill first?"

Ashlyn refilled my cup and then pointed to the toast. "I mean it, Em. Eat it all. You'll thank me later."

If I wasn't puking it up, that is. But I recognized this mood and Ashlyn wasn't going to give in. I took a bite and chewed.

She stood across the island from me wearing a determined expression and drinking her own coffee. She placed it on the counter before speaking.

"Okay, here it is. I usually don't have to tell you anything because you're always saying and doing the right thing but clearly you need an intervention. First, getting drunk last night was kind of stupid. I can see why you did it but dragging Shelby into it was not something a friend would do. She's got all sorts of issues she needs to deal with. She was with Brad for years and she's not going to get over him in a few days."

"Like I should? Because Owen and I didn't date very long?"

I sounded more aggressive than I meant to but she'd basically just said that I didn't have anything to be upset about.

"That's from your own lips, babe. You said yourself it was too soon for you to be in love. Are you taking that back?"

No. Maybe.

"I don't need any advice–"

"Yes, you do and you need it badly." Ashlyn reached across the granite counter and patted my hand. "I've always known you were a little gun shy when it came to men and frankly none of us were concerned. We always assumed that when you found the right one, you'd figure it out. You're so smart, after all. But that's not what happened. That's when I realized that love doesn't have a thing to do with being intelligent. It's about your heart, and you don't have a scintilla of experience listening to that organ. You've given your brain far too much control, Em. It stops today."

I was way too hungover to take this shit.

"I think–"

She waved away my rebuttal. "That's your problem, Em. You're always thinking. There are times when your brain is going to get you in trouble. This is one of them. Because there is no logical reason to fall in love, my friend. There is no logical reason to ever trust another human being. But we do it anyway. We do it against all evidence because our hearts tell us to."

I tried to open my mouth to speak but she held up her hand and shook her head.

"You'll get to speak when I'm done. I know what you're thinking. You're thinking that if you followed your heart all the time, you'd be a brokenhearted mess. Well…sometimes that happens. Sometimes we misjudge and we get a slap-down in return." Her expression softened and she patted my hand again. "And I know that you've had more than your share of that. I know that you've tried to believe but life has knocked you down more times than you can count. You're battered, bruised, and exhausted. But being a human in this world means you have to get back up again. You have to fight."

I wanted to but she was right. I was tired.

"Why can't it be easy?"

I hadn't even realized I was speaking until the words were out. More like a whine than an actual statement.

"Because nothing worth it ever is," she sighed. "It's sucks, doesn't it? But that's the way. Look at Mia and Josh or me and Kyle. It didn't come easily. We had to fight for our happily ever after and you do, too."

"Shelby and Brad–"

"Don't," she said sharply. "Don't go there. Shelby ignored warning sign after warning sign. We saw it and didn't say a word. We're complicit. But you are not Shelby and Owen is not Brad."

We were guilty and would have to live with that.

"I wanted to take a chance with Owen. I tried to do that. Just like Shelby's book said to."

Understanding crossed Ashlyn's features. "You took advice from Shelby and then when her relationship fell apart it gave you doubts. That explains so much. Shelby is probably the one person on the planet whose advice you would actually listen to."

That wasn't true.

"Uh...I'm kind of listening to you now."

"You have to admit that's not your usual *modus operandi.*"

"Are you calling me a know-it-all?"

"Yes," Ashlyn answered with a kind smile. "But only in the nicest and sweetest way."

Sometimes I wished my friends would lie to me more often.

"I'm not sure one can be a sweet know-it-all but thank you for that." I paused and took another fortifying sip of my coffee. Slowly but surely, I was beginning to feel more human-like. "I do like to be right."

"You do, but then I guess we all do. Your need is simply stronger. I've always put that down to your childhood."

"Middle child syndrome? You sound like Shelby."

And Owen.

"I'll take that as a compliment, and yes, middle child syndrome. You were praised for being practical, efficient, and smart. That's not a bad thing but I think in your mind you might have taken it a bit too far. You seem to think that those are your best qualities."

"They are my best qualities. It sure isn't my singing."

Ashlyn slapped her hand over her mouth and laughed. "You are a terrible singer but efficiency is not your best quality."

Okay, I'll bite. She wanted me to ask, obviously.

"What is my best quality?"

"Your heart. Your warm, loving, and generous heart. You stomp around with that resting bitch face scaring everyone in your path but you're actually a teddy bear filled with fluff. You want people to think you're formidable, and you are, but you're also the best friend anyone could ever hope to have. I know that if I called in the middle of the night and told you to bring a shovel, you'd bury the body and we'd never speak of it again."

Shit, now I was all choked up with tears. I didn't want to cry.

"Even now," Ashlyn went on, "you don't want to show any weakness. It's okay if you want to shed a tear or two. I won't tell anyone."

"So what you're basically saying is that I'm a freakin' mess. If I were a man, I'd want to stay far away from me. I don't have a clue as to what to do or how to act."

"I think Owen, or any guy for that matter, would be lucky to have you love him. Because you're the type that once you fall in love, that will be it. It's forever."

In the time that Owen and I had been together I'd begun to believe that as well.

"I wanted to love Owen. I wanted…to believe in him. And us." I stood, wanting to fill my empty coffee cup. "But I don't know anything about this magic of love. I don't think I know anything about love at all. I'm love-deficient."

"That's where you are wrong. The fact that you wanted to set aside your cynicism for Owen and believe in the two of you is a huge step. I've never heard you talk like that before. See? The magic even worked on you."

Had it? I didn't feel any different. If you didn't count the horrible hangover I currently had. But…

"It doesn't matter anyway. It's too late. He's with her and he's happy."

Ashlyn lifted the coffee cup out of my hand just as I was going to reach for the still warm pot. "Do you hear yourself? Emerson Grant never gives in or gracefully accepts defeat. She fights for what she wants. She takes chances. Like when you opened your business. Everyone told you that you'd regret it but you made them eat their words. It's time to take another chance."

That sounded scarier than jumping out of a plane with only

a tiny parachute.

"I'm not sure I can do that."

"I know that you can," Ashlyn replied firmly. "You'll never have what you want unless you take a chance. Do you want Owen?"

"Yes."

"Then you're going to have to go after him. What's the worst thing that could happen?"

Holy hell, did she really just ask that question?

"Complete and utter humiliation."

I wasn't sure I could handle Owen turning away from me, telling me that he didn't love me after all.

"You're already hungover from drinking too much because of him. Really, when you think about it, you've hit rock bottom. There's no way to go but up."

"There's another woman," I pointed out. "What about her?"

"What about her?" Ashlyn shot back. "He can't be in love with her because he told you that. Maybe she's a friend or a coworker. Maybe she's a rebound, but he can't have deep feelings for her. If he does, then you're better off without him. Is he the type of guy who flits from female to female?"

No, he wasn't which made last night all the more strange.

"He was pretty mad when he walked out. I doubt he'd take my call."

Scrunching up her face, Ashlyn thought for a moment. "We're going to need a plan. You need to do something big to show him that you're sincere. Like how I flew to Seattle to be with Kyle."

"My brain isn't working well right now. I can't think of

anything."

"I can. I know just what you can do."

Ashlyn and I both whirled around when we heard that voice. Shelby. She was standing in the kitchen doorway looking only slightly better than myself.

"How long have you been standing there?" I asked. "You're sneaky."

Shelby stepped farther into the room, holding onto the island for support. "Long enough to know that you need a big gesture. I can help with that. I have an idea."

I was always afraid when Shelby had ideas. Everyone was. I was also desperate enough to do it.

"Let's hear it," Ashlyn said, reaching for another cup in the cabinet. "Do you want some toast to go with your coffee?"

"We need the usual hangover remedy," Shelby said, authority in her tone. "What time does the diner open?"

My stomach lurched at the mere thought of what Shelby was talking about. She thought hangovers could be cured with greasy diner food. Lots of it.

"It's open now," Ashlyn replied. "I'll give them a call. What else are we going to need?"

I feared this answer. Great fear.

"I'll go into it as soon as I've showered and eaten." Shelby looked at me. "Are you in?"

Yes. I wanted a chance with Owen, even if it meant more heartbreak. And diner food.

"I'm in. But I do have a question."

Shelby accepted the coffee cup from Ashlyn. "Shoot."

"Does anyone know where my shoes are?"

CHAPTER TWENTY-EIGHT

Owen

TERI, AN ADMIN, poked her head into my office interrupting my afternoon of doing absolutely nothing. I'd been about as productive as a statue today.

"Dr, Shelby Kelly is on line two. Do you want me to take a message?"

I'd basically told Teri that I didn't want to talk or see anyone today. I wasn't in the best of moods even after Carly had set me straight last night. Fear didn't put me in the best of moods and I was terrified. I was going to call Emmy tonight and ask her to see me so we could talk.

If she didn't hang up on me. Carly assured me that I had a good chance of patching things up. I hoped she was correct.

This was interesting, though. Shelby had called the office on occasion but not often. Did this have to do with Emmy? My heart dropped to my stomach. Was she okay? Had something happened?

"I'll take that call, Teri. Put her through. Thanks."

"Owen? Hi, this is Shelby."

I cradled the phone between my ear and shoulder, my heart still beating like a bass drum in a marching band. "Hi, Shelby.

What can I do for you?"

I'd wanted to ask straight out if Emmy was okay but I didn't even know if that was why Shelby was calling. Maybe she simply wanted me to pen the forward to the book Emmy had talked about.

"I know this is last minute but I'm hoping you can help me. I really need to talk to you. Do you think we could meet for a drink?"

I couldn't contain the question. I needed to know. "Is this about Emmy? Is she okay?"

"She's fine," Shelby answered swiftly. "I mean, she's upset, of course, but she's fine. No, this is about me and my...situation."

I could breathe easier knowing that Emmy wasn't hurt or sick.

If this didn't have anything to do with Emmy then it appeared that Shelby wanted to speak to me in a professional capacity. Did she want to talk or perhaps she wanted to use my dating service? Either way I would help her. She'd been through the wringer in the last week or so.

"Of course, I'll meet you for a drink. You name the place and time."

"Why don't we meet at the fountain downtown? There are several places near there. About six?"

"Perfect. I'll be there."

Then I'd go home and call Emmy.

Emmy

I WAS SWEATING through my blouse, a sheer black number with pink polka dots. I was wearing it over a black camisole that was currently sticking to my back and making me uncomfortable. The temperature of the bar was damn near freezing but I was still *glowing* as Ashlyn liked to call it. At this rate, I was going to look like I'd jumped in a lake with my clothes on.

"I'm so fucking nervous," I said through gritted teeth. Otherwise they'd chatter from complete and total terror. "Why did I ever tell Shelby about my date here with Owen? Better question… Why did I agree to do this?"

Ashlyn handed me a bottle of water. I'd begged for booze but she'd said that I needed to keep a clear head. Bitch. She was probably right but I could have used a shot of whiskey right about now.

I was off tequila for awhile after last night.

"Because you want Owen to see that you've changed," she explained patiently. "That you're willing to take chances."

"It's those people in the audience that will have taken the big chance when I start belting out a tune. They'll cover their ears and run screaming from the building."

Ashlyn simply smiled and patted my shoulder. "As long as Owen stays then it's okay."

"I might make the news. I can see the headlines now. *Local woman's singing forces audience to gouge out their eardrums. People flee to the hills.*"

"We're in the middle of the prairie. There are no hills."

She was right. The biggest hill we had was in the park and people sled down it when it snowed but no one was going to be able to hide in it. Or even behind it.

I took a big gulp of water. "It's going to be fine."

"Of course, it is. I wouldn't let you do anything stupid. You're my friend."

"If you're my friend, explain to me how I got here again because I still can't believe that I agreed to this."

This was the karaoke bar that Owen and I had visited with Lisa and Dan.

The plan was that Shelby would lure Owen here on the pretense of needing his professional advice.

The action was that I would go up onstage and sing a love song dedicated to Owen despite the fact that I sounded like a cat dying in an alley.

The hoped result was that he would be so overwhelmed by my stupidity that he'd give our relationship another chance.

Hey, it worked in the movies…

When Shelby had described her little plan, I had been wholeheartedly against it. There simply had to be another way. I'd proposed showing up at his house with dinner and wine, asking him if we could talk but both Ashlyn and Shelby had been horrified by that suggestion.

What if he had a female there?

I could call first?

Shelby insisted that I had to make a grand gesture to show how much I've changed. To show that the magic of love had done its work on me, too. Eventually they'd worn me down so here I was, standing in the wings of the stage waiting for Owen to show up.

And seriously thinking about fleeing for those hills I'd mentioned earlier. This was not going to go well. Owen was going to think I'd lost my mind and the only thing that was going to come from this was I'd be barred from all karaoke bars for a hundred-mile radius.

Ashlyn pointed to a table on the other side of the room. "There he is. Owen and Shelby have arrived. I'll let the manager know you're ready."

But I wasn't ready. Not at all.

Pressing a hand to my chest, I could feel my heart racing underneath the palm. My stomach was doing a Cirque de Soleil number in my abdomen and I was heartily glad that lunch was many hours ago. It might have made an impromptu appearance.

Woman pukes onstage. Film at eleven.

Finally working up the courage, I turned to look at Owen who was speaking animatedly to Shelby. He hadn't yet noticed me and he probably wouldn't. Ashlyn had found the darkest corner of this joint and from the angle that we were sitting at he'd have to crane his neck to get a glimpse of me. But I could watch him right now and he'd never know.

It had been less than forty-eight hours but I missed him. He looked the same as always, dressed in casual denims and a button down shirt. His silky hair just brushed the collar and I wanted to reach out and wind my fingers through it. Owen had been complaining that he needed a haircut but I liked it.

Currently his head was bent close to Shelby's, intently listening to whatever bullshit she was telling him. She'd said something about asking him for advice about Brad and he seemed to be giving it, nodding and speaking every now and then.

"Okay, you're up." Ashlyn had left and come back already. "He's going to announce you and then you can get the plan rolling."

"I think I'm going to be sick."

Ashlyn simply smiled and pulled me out of my chair. My knees buckled and I had to hold onto the table. "You can be sick later. There's no time right now. It's begun."

I'd used those exact words on several brides who were about to walk down the aisle. They'd take one look at the full church and get spooked, declaring that they were going to throw up. I'd always said that the best thing to do was be calm and in control and tell them that they could do that later.

It was too late to make a run for it. I was going to do this because I wanted Owen to know that I could, indeed, take a chance.

It's begun.

★ ★ ★

Owen

A KARAOKE BAR was a strange place to have a relationship discussion but Shelby had been adamant about the location, saying that the odds of seeing anyone she knew were low. She was avoiding people in general as they seemed to ask personal and embarrassing questions she didn't want to answer. Frankly, it was none of their damn business but even well-meaning folks could be a pain in the ass.

I'd ordered a beer and Shelby a cranberry juice. Over the drinks, she'd confessed that she'd known for quite awhile that her relationship with Brad wasn't on firm footing but she'd ignored it, hoping that it would solve itself. Unfortunately, these issues rarely do.

That's why I needed to speak with Emmy. We had differences that we needed to work on but they weren't fatal to our relationship. Yes, they were frustrating, and I shouldn't have let it get to me the other night, but if we worked together we could get through it. A little compromise on both our parts would go a long way. I wanted her to know that I could be patient.

"I think you just need to give yourself time, Shelby. It hasn't been–"

"Look, someone is about to sing," she broke in, her gaze on the stage. She fidgeted in her chair and craned her neck. "Is that…Emmy? I think it is."

What in the hell?

I hadn't been paying any attention to the stage or anyone around us, but now every cell in my being was zoned directly in on the lone woman standing on stage. Just her and the microphone.

Emmy.

My breath caught in my chest as I gazed at her. She looked beautiful, but then she always did. She was dressed in a black pencil skirt, black blouse, and black high heels. I could just see the curve of her ankles and calves and damn if it wasn't sexier than if she'd been standing there stark naked. Her hair was down, tumbling around her shoulders, and her lips quivered with fear. Even from this distance I could see that she was frozen with fear, her eyes wide and her lips quivering.

Christ on a crutch, what was she doing? She'd told me that she couldn't sing, that she was so terrible she could crack glass. What would make her stand up in front of a crowd – okay, a half-full bar – and sing? It didn't make a lick of sense.

"She wants you to know that she's willing to take a chance."

Shelby's soft voice interrupted my thoughts but I couldn't pull my attention from Emmy. I wanted to run up on stage and wrap her in my arms, telling her that everything would be okay. She was absolutely scared out of her mind.

Emmy took a shaky step forward to stand in front of the microphone as the manager announced that they had a special guest singer tonight who wanted to dedicate a song.

Clearing her throat, she squinted against the lights shining in her eyes. "I'm singing this song for Owen."

Holy fuck. I didn't need Emmy to do this. I already loved her.

"What was she thinking? She can't sing."

Shelby nodded toward the stage. "She wanted to show you that she can take a crazy chance and I suggested this one."

This time I did turn to Shelby, leaning down so she wouldn't miss a word of what I had to say. "Shelby, you're a brilliant psychologist and a good person but this is possibly the worst idea that anyone has ever had anywhere, anyplace, at any time."

I didn't wait for her reaction, shoving my chair back and getting to my feet. Striding up to the stage, I could hear the first notes of "Hopelessly Devoted to You" being played and I could only pray that I reached her before she began to sing.

"Emmy, you don't have to do this."

I stopped inches from where she stood on stage. Surprise, hope, relief, and then tenderness all flitted across her features. I should never have doubted myself. I'd seen her love. It was there even if she didn't shout it to everyone in Arborville. She might be scared of it but that didn't make it any less present.

"You don't have to do this," I repeated. The song was still playing but the crowd had quieted down, sensing that something interesting was going on. "I love you, Emmy."

Her hands flew to her mouth and tears sparkled in her eyes. Sniffling, she took my hand as I stepped up on the stage with her.

"I love you, too."

The microphone was so close that her statement was blared out of the speakers for all to hear. A collective cheer went up from the patrons but I didn't give a shit. I just wanted her.

"I wanted to do something risky, something to show you that I understand."

The crowd could still hear us but all I could see was this amazing woman who was willing to do dumb shit just for me. I was ready to do anything and everything for her. She didn't even need to ask.

"Understand what, honey?"

She smiled at that moment, a little shaky and scared, but it still had the power to jerk the heart in my chest to life. These last two days I'd been only existing.

"The magic of love. I know that it's real now because it's changed me."

I shook my head and ran my hands up her arms, coming to rest on her shoulders. "You never needed to change. I needed to be more patient. Honey, you're wonderful just the way you are."

"I need to be–"

"Exactly what you are," I said, not letting her finish. "Efficient, practical, bossy, beautiful, loving, and the woman of my heart. I got impatient and greedy and I wanted it all on my timetable. I won't make that mistake again."

The patrons in the bar were going wild now, screaming and hollering, stomping their feet. I could hear exhortations to kiss her, ask her to marry me, and a few other suggestions that were definitely on the X-rated side. I'd save those for when we were alone.

"We're both going to make mistakes, Owen. I know I will and you probably will, too. I think we'll react differently next time. Stay and fight it out instead of walking away."

"No more walking away. We stay and work it out," I vowed, pulling her closer. "I don't suppose you have any ideas as to how we can make a graceful exit off of this stage?"

Wrinkling her nose, she shook her head. "Nope, the girls talked me into getting up here but they never told me how to get down. I think they were depending on you to know what to do."

I only knew one thing to do. I'd seen it in a movie.

Bending down, I placed my arm under Emmy's knees and lifted her into my arms. For a moment, I thought I might be too much of a weakling to carry this plan off but then she was settled against my chest and it wasn't bad at all.

"Emmy, I love you. Let's give this a try."

"I love you too, and I say yes."

She was smiling at me, and even in this light I could see the love shining out of her eyes. It wouldn't be easy. Emmy and I had strong personalities and there were going to be times that we disagreed. We simply had to keep our eye on what was important.

The magic of love.

I hope you enjoyed Owen and Emmy's story! Shelby's story will be coming soon.

Thank you for reading Touch Him.

Don't miss a thing! Sign up to be notified of Olivia's new releases:

www.OliviaJaymes.com

About The Author

Olivia Jaymes is a wife, mother, lover of sexy romance, and caffeine addict. She lives with her husband and son in central Florida and spends her days with handsome alpha males and spunky heroines.

She is currently working on a new contemporary romance series – *Man Trap* in addition to her other ongoing series.

Visit Olivia Jaymes at

www.OliviaJaymes.com

Other Titles by Olivia Jaymes

Danger Incorporated

Damsel In Danger

Hiding From Danger

Discarded Heart Novella

Indecent Danger

Embracing Danger

Danger In The Night

Reunited With Danger

Window to Danger

Road to Danger

Unwanted Danger

Cowboy Justice Association

Cowboy Command

Justice Healed

Cowboy Truth

Cowboy Famous

Cowboy Cool

Imperfect Justice

The Deputies

Justice Inked

Justice Reborn

Vengeful Justice

Justice Divided

Seeking Justice

Military Moguls

Champagne and Bullets

Diamonds and Revolvers

Caviar and Covert Ops

Emeralds, Rubies, and Camouflage

Midnight Blue Beach

Wicked After Midnight

Midnight Of No Return

Kiss Midnight Goodbye

The Hollywood Showmance Chronicles

A Kiss For the Cameras

Swinging From A Star

Wild on the Red Carpet

Love in the Spotlight

And the Winner is

Man Trap

Tempt Him

Tease Him

Touch Him

www.ingramcontent.com/pod-product-compliance
Lightning Source LLC
Chambersburg PA
CBHW030959260626
47169CB00002B/605
* 9 7 8 1 9 4 4 4 9 0 5 3 9 *